1980

A Year in the Life of Keith Diamond

By Jason Ayres

if it wasn't for his minor celebrity status, it was unlikely that any woman would look twice at him.

It had reached the point where few did in any case. He found the rules of modern dating difficult and soon he might not even have his fame to fall back on. Every day he felt as if he were swimming against the tide in an increasingly hostile media environment full of enemies who would like nothing more than to see him taken off the air – permanently. Lately, they had taken to dredging up every controversial remark he had ever made in the past and plastering it all over Twitter.

As he got up from the desk he nearly knocked over his coffee mug from which his own face was beaming back at him. It was an image that was somewhat flattering in comparison with reality, but then the mug was a few years old. It was a leftover from some merchandise he had invested in to flog at roadshows. He had ordered 3,000 of them and they displayed his image with the words *The Diamond Geezer – You know he talks sense* emblazoned across the front. They hadn't sold as well as he had hoped and he still had a box with several hundred of them left in the spare room of his two-bedroom flat in Fulham. Recently, he had hit on the wheeze of awarding them as prizes to listeners to the show but it was still hard to get rid of them, even for free. Often the callers rang off hurriedly before leaving their address.

The rest of the desk was messy with various notes, bits of stationery, and half-eaten food left by the presenter who had been on the graveyard shift before him. It was bloody inconsiderate of her not to clean it up, in his opinion. He hated mess, a throwback to sharing a flat with his fellow journalist Jimmy, when they had first come to London long ago. The studio in general was looking rather jaded with walls adorned with faded photographs of famous guests who had graced the studio – some politicians, some entertainers, and even one of Keith himself from a couple of decades ago when he could just about still have passed as a poster boy.

The studio was perched high up within a skyscraper, with the window behind his desk boasting a bird's-eye view of the city's landmarks, from Big Ben to the London Eye. But Keith didn't have time to admire the scenery. He needed to get to the toilet.

He had to get up and go frequently during the show as he had been having some bladder difficulties recently. He seemed to be going every fifteen minutes and even then he couldn't get it all out. As soon as he popped the little fella back into his pants, the pressure squeezed out a couple more drops. He didn't know if this was a problem all men had as they got older or if there was something wrong with him, but he was unlikely to find out as the one thing the Diamond Geezer didn't do was doctors. His long-dead mentor Ted, from his early days on the tabloids, had told him so many horror stories about the medical profession that it had put him off for life.

Not that these avoidance tactics had done old Ted any good in the end but even so, the distrust of doctors had stayed with him. There was also the fear that there really was something seriously wrong with him. But his dubious logic dictated that if he didn't know, then he couldn't worry about it. Provided he maintained his personal hygiene, it would not be a problem. The most

Contents

December 2019

"Wakey wakey, Britain, and I mean that in more ways than one! It's 7 o'clock on this chilly December morning, indeed, the last one of the year! Where did 2019 go, eh? You're tuned into the Big Bad Breakfast Show here on ChatFM with me, Keith Diamond, or as you all know and love me, the Diamond GEEZER!"

Keith delivered his self-appointed nickname as he always did – at a volume loud enough to rouse any dozing listeners who were reluctant to get out of bed, and in the exaggerated fake cockney accent he had developed over the years. It was all part of the persona he had fabricated, the salt-of-the-earth, East End lad made good. He saw it as his mission in life to champion the cause of the beleaguered Londoner, besieged by the trials and tribulations of the modern world from every angle. What most of his listeners didn't know was that he had been born and bred in Watford.

"And, as always we've got a jam-packed show lined up for you today, with lashings of common sense to go with your bacon and eggs. If we're still allowed to have that for breakfast, of course. We won't be able to for much longer when the militant vegans get their way, eh? Anyway, first up, we're going to talk about Brexit. Is Boris going to get it done? We're also going to be talking about the green agenda. What's going on with that? The rest of the media are obsessed with it. Saving the planet? Don't make me laugh. Who's going to pay for it all? I'll tell you who! Me and you, Muggins the taxpayer!"

Keith paused for breath, pleased with the way his opening monologue was going. Muggins the taxpayer was one of his favourite catchphrases for riling up the audience. And he had plenty more where that came from.

"Later, we've got a guy coming on who has been working on tonight's annual firework display, and get this. It's going woke! Yes, our beloved mayor has decided we're having a politically correct fireworks display. How's that going to work? Well, I guess we'll see tonight but you can get a sneak preview here first, on the biggest, baddest breakfast show in Britain. You just don't get quality broadcasting like this anywhere else! But before we get into all that, it's time to cross to the newsroom and get you up to speed with the morning headlines."

Keith flicked the microphone off and hauled himself up out of the seat, knowing he had just three minutes to get to the toilet and back. At sixty-two, with a long career in journalism behind him, he was a man who'd enjoyed more than his fair share of large lunches, and his figure showed it – or rather, the straining seams of his ill-fitting blue suit did. His face bore the signs of a lifetime of heavy drinking, his chubby cheeks flecked with red patches and bloodshot, tired eyes that had barely seen a decent night's sleep since he had first arrived in Fleet Street over forty years ago.

His hair was thinning, just a few wispy grey strands left of the curly black locks that had turned plenty of heads back in the day. Then, with his natural charisma and charm he had taken full advantage and enjoyed a very active sex life. But those days were long past. Now, important thing was remembering to change his trousers twice a day as it only took a few hours before they started to stink of stale piss.

He had seen some male incontinence products advertised on television. These were normally shown alongside commercials for erectile dysfunction products or insurance for funeral expenses that came with the enticing offer of a free Parker pen. Presumably, these ads were aimed at retired folk who had nothing better to do than watch television all day. Well, he wasn't as old as them yet, and there was no way he was going to be wearing nappies again any time soon. Provided he arrived at the studio fresh from the shower wearing newly laundered clothes, then he was reasonably confident nobody would notice. And they hadn't so far. At least he didn't think they had.

While he was at the urinal his producer, Tom, was in his headphones badgering him to get back, but he ignored him. He knew exactly how long he had. First the news, then the weather, then an ad, usually for some fast-food company or other. He had four minutes precisely, and as always was back in his seat with a few seconds to spare. In his absence his first guest, a prominent Tory MP, had arrived and was waiting for him on the other side of his desk.

"Right then, without further ado, let's get into it, and no prizes for guessing what our first topic is. Yes, it's Brexit again! I know you think I keep banging on about it, but come on. It's been three and a half years of faffing about and we still don't know if we're getting a hard Brexit, a soft Brexit, or a three-bags-full Brexit. It's time to put these ministers on the spot, and I'm pleased to say,

I've got one right here and I'm going to ask him the questions the others won't. They don't get an easy ride here like they do on those other stations, you know, the ones we don't talk about. And don't forget you can call tweet or text, and you never know, you might even get on the show. Remember, the best caller of the day wins a free Diamond Geezer mug!"

And then he was away, in full flow, conducting his first interview of the day. It didn't take long for the calls and tweets to come flooding in. He knew exactly how to press the right buttons to stir up controversy. The truth was, he couldn't give a toss about Brexit, immigration, or any of the other topics he liked to bang on about. He hadn't even bothered to vote in the referendum; he just found it amusing how seriously both the remainers and the leavers took it all, and enjoyed stirring them up, like a small boy poking at ants in a nest.

By the time the first twenty-minute segment of the show was complete, Keith needed the toilet again, and as usual his producer wouldn't shut up while he was trying desperately to go. But today, there was something noticeably different about Tom's tone of voice. When he informed him that he had been summoned to the station manager's office immediately after the show, Keith felt an unusual sense of foreboding.

He had been frogmarched upstairs many times in the past for overstepping the mark, but as far as he knew he hadn't done anything particularly controversial so far this week. He was more concerned about some of the rumours that had been flying around the station about a possible takeover. That could put his position in jeopardy.

The broadcasting company occupied the whole of the 64th and 65th floors of the high-rise tower, and it was just a short lift ride up to the management suite on the floor above. But when he entered the boss's office, he was in for a shock.

There was no sign of Douglas, the grumpy old git whom Keith was more than capable of running rings around every time he tried to scold him for some perceived misdemeanour. Instead, he was confronted by an impeccably dressed lady in a tailored charcoal suit, her attire a sharp contrast to Keith's rumpled appearance. He was embarrassingly aware that while he had been interviewing the MP, one of the buttons had given up the unequal battle against his expanding blubber and popped off. It had exposed his hairy midriff and his tie wasn't long enough to cover it.

"Who are you?" he asked warily. "Where's Douglas?"

"Gone," she said, looking him straight in the eye. As he met her gaze, he perceived an uncomfortable gulf between his scruffy demeanour and her polished appearance. Not only was she immaculately dressed, but she was well groomed too, most notably with her shiny chestnut curls cascading freely over her shoulders. She radiated not just confidence but power, and suddenly this familiar office, so often a battleground between him and Douglas in the past where he invariably came out on top, now felt as hostile as an away game at Millwall.

"You don't remember me, do you?" she asked.

"Should I?" asked Keith, before slipping into his usual modus operandi and adding, "I've been around a long time. I can't be expected to remember every woman I've… encountered, can I?"

Although he said this in his usual manner, he chose his words carefully. He didn't add love or darling to the end of the sentence, though he couldn't resist leaving a little pause before the word 'encountered', just to allude to the possibility he might have dallied with her between the sheets at some point in the past.

"Oh, there's no reason why you should, considering how little you thought of me the last time we met. In fact, I don't think you even saw me as an actual person at all. Just someone to objectify."

Bloody hell, thought Keith, *not again*. He'd had all this on Twitter a while back with some woman he swore he couldn't remember who insisted on adding the hashtag #MeToo to all her posts about him. He had dismissed it, reminding his followers that social media was not real life. But now it was being said right to his face and it made for an uncomfortable situation.

"Well, it was all a long time ago, probably," he said, crossing his arms defensively as he racked his brains trying to picture where he had seen her before and drawing a blank.

"You're right, it was," she replied. "Almost forty years, as it happens."

"Really?" said Keith, looking at the woman who to his eye couldn't be older than early fifties at the most. "You must have been very young."

"Oh, I was," she said. "Fifteen, to be precise. Cast your mind back to 1980. Fleet Street. Do you remember what you were doing?"

"Sure," he said. "I have very fond memories of those times. I was just starting out in journalism and had landed my first role on one of the tabloids. But you can't have been there, surely?"

"Oh, I was. I came to Fleet Street to do my week's work experience. I was keen on a media career and managed to get the paper to take me for a week. I thought it was going to be an inspiring introduction to the world of journalism. Instead, it was a week of sheer hell."

"It can't have been the same paper I was working on. Those were halcyon days, brilliant fun. Nothing like the bloody miserable state of the world now. Perhaps you just weren't cut out for it at such a tender age."

"I'll say," she replied. "That newsroom was the most disgusting, misogynistic place I have been in my entire life. A room dominated by white, sexist men, constantly smoking, frequently drunk, and leering at the few women employees, who were inevitably only in administration roles. And you and your mate, Jimmy, were two of the worst."

"Ah, good old Jimmy. He's still around, you know."

"Oh, yes, I know. I've listened to the podcast you two do together. Absolute filth. Neither of you has changed a bit."

"Our podcast isn't bound by Ofcom rules, unlike this station at which, I hasten to add, I adhere to those rules. But on the podcast, we can say what we like."

"What, like last week when you were comparing notes on which politicians you'd like to shag? And you said that you wanted to give Theresa May one."

"That was a joke. Obviously, I don't want to. I was just trying to shock the listeners. Now, Liz Truss, on the other hand…"

"You see, this is exactly what I am talking about. You have not changed one iota since 1980. That office was poison, pure poison."

"Look, much as I'm enjoying this trip down memory lane," said Keith, who wasn't enjoying it at all, "you still haven't told me who you are."

"My name is Nathalie Dupont," she said.

"Nope, still doesn't ring any bells. Dupont, that's a French name, isn't it?"

"My father was French, my mother was English," replied Nathalie. "So, even though I've told you my name, you still don't remember me. And you don't even know who I am now, in today's world?"

"Nope," said Keith.

"Remarkable," said Nathalie. "Let me fill you in on both fronts. Clearly, you remember nothing of the week I spent in the newsroom in 1980. As soon as I got there, you and your mates started wolf-whistling, making lewd comments, and refusing to give me any proper work experience at all other than making tea."

"That's just how things were, back then," said Keith, in a lame attempt to justify the unjustifiable. "I didn't create the office that way, that was just the environment I came into, barely a year before you. And from what little I recall we didn't even want work experience kids there but we had to do it as a favour to the local school because Jerry, my old boss, was knocking off the deputy head."

"That sums up that world in a nutshell. Everything was governed by sex and money and controlled by the men. And from the way you talk, I can only conclude that you think the world still works like that. Well, I'm sorry, it doesn't, and you simply can't go around saying the sort of things that you do anymore."

"I can say whatever I like. I'm the Diamond Geezer," he replied rather weakly, his usual arrogance subdued as he knew she was getting the upper hand. It felt like a poker game where he needed to go all-in to survive and had been dealt a 2 and a 7 – the worst possible hand.

"Yes, well we'll come on to that. Anyway, you and Jimmy kept going on about my tits. He said he wanted to put me on Page 3 and kept asking how long until I was sixteen. While you made it quite clear what you wanted to give me for my sixteenth birthday present."

"Oh, I'm sure that was just harmless banter, we wouldn't have meant anything by it."

"Harmless banter? So you think it's acceptable for two grown men to talk that way to a fifteen-year-old girl?"

"I was barely much more than a kid myself, fresh out of university. It was a different time and I was young and immature. That of course, is if things happened the way you claim they did because I don't remember any of this. Are you sure it wasn't just your precocious teenage hormones making you overly sensitive? Or you're deliberately embellishing the facts retrospectively just so you can jump on the latest man-hating bandwagon?"

"No, and I'll thank you not to talk down to me like that. The assaults weren't just verbal, they were physical too. I'm guessing you're going to say that you don't remember pinching me on the bottom, either?"

"No, I don't. I've never done that to any woman so I wouldn't go trying to make out that I have now."

He felt confident in saying that. He knew others in the office had done it, but he had never been one of them.

"Well, I say you did," she insisted.

"Got any evidence? I doubt it. Unlike today, where you can't say or do anything without the risk of someone filming or recording your every word, there is no record of anything that happened back then. If someone did do that, then it was probably Gordon or Bob. They were both a little handsy from what I recall. I can assure you with one hundred per cent certainty that it was not me, so try and make an issue of this now and I'll call you out on it. I've got a lot of followers on social media who'll take my side, love, don't you worry."

He thought he had fought his corner well with this latest comeback but she showed no sign of being rattled. Her posture remained poised and unwavering, and her tone steady, as she spoke slowly, each word dripping with an underlying sense of control.

"Never refer to me as love, sweetheart, flower, or any other outdated patronising term. Not that we'll be having any further contact after today because do you know what I vowed to myself all those years ago?"

"What? To stop playing with your Barbies and face up to the real world?" Keith knew he had nothing to lose now, so decided he might as well revert to type, even though he knew his response was a cheap and lame jibe.

"No. That nobody was ever going to get away with treating me that way again. I swore that I was going to work my socks off in the hope that one day, the boot would be well and truly on the other foot so that you and others like you would get your comeuppance for what you did to me all those years ago. Well that boot's fully strapped on and ready to connect with your arse."

Keith didn't want to give her the satisfaction of an easy win so he huffed dismissively and grinned as if this was all some big joke. No way was he showing her that he was upset by this turn of events. What was it she had said at the start about Douglas being gone? He was keen to learn what had happened to his former boss.

"Is it now? And what's Douglas got to say about all this?"

"Not a lot, I would imagine. His feet didn't touch the floor on the way out. You can't tell me you haven't figured out what's going on here, surely? I know your Diamond Geezer persona on the radio comes across as being as thick as two short planks but I assumed that was just part of your act. Now, I'm beginning to wonder."

"Just spit it out, will you," said Keith, who was getting bored with this charade and felt it was time to get the inevitable over with.

"Right, well, as of first thing this morning, ChatFM as an independent entity has ceased to exist. We've bought the whole thing, lock, stock, and barrel."

"And who is 'we' exactly?"

13

"Rainbow Media," she said, smirking, anticipating his response with glee.

"You must be joking!" replied Keith incredulously. "Rainbow Media? What on earth would you want with a right-leaning radio station?"

"Well, that's just it. The politics of this station are bigoted, outdated rubbish, and there is no place for it in the progressive broadcasting world. We're going to bring the content more in line with modern values."

"You mean you're going to sing from the same hymn sheet as all the others? It'll be just another BBC or LBC, and who wants that?"

"We do," she said. "And I'm sure I don't need to tell you what that means for you."

"You're sacking me?" he said, feigning surprise. "Really? My listeners will never stand for it."

"I do not need to sack you. I know you've been here for nearly a decade but I'm sure I don't need to remind you that you are not an employee of this station. You are self-employed and have always been paid by the shift. Which means we have no obligation to you whatsoever. You're only as good as your last show which, I'm sure you won't be surprised to hear, finished about twenty minutes ago. And the best thing of all is we don't have to pay you a penny of redundancy money."

Nathalie's lips curved into a brief victorious smirk as she delivered her killer blow. Her face and poise glowed with smug satisfaction as if she had been waiting for this moment for decades. Which, indeed, she had.

"This is all a bit sad really, isn't it, Nathalie?" said Keith. "This isn't about business at all, is it? It's all about the poor little girl who got her feelings hurt forty years ago and has been bearing a grudge ever since. Have you really spent half a lifetime consumed with a desire for revenge? That's not healthy, you know."

"No, this is purely a professional decision. It doesn't fit our business model to have sexist and racist presenters on our channels."

"Whoa, hold up a moment. You can't throw accusations like that about. Name one racist thing I have ever said or written."

Nathalie didn't reply.

"You can't because I haven't and I'm not. I could sue you just for saying that."

"This is a private conversation, so unless you're recording it, good luck. But from the way you bang on about immigration all the time on your show, it's plain obvious what you think."

"I can assure you, I do not think that. This station is about free speech and debating issues. That's all."

"Well, not anymore it isn't."

"Of course it isn't. Because people like you don't want to debate issues. You want everyone to think exactly the same way you do and woe betide anyone who doesn't toe the line. And you have the cheek to bang on about diversity all the time. What about diversity of opinion?"

"You're quite free to express your opinions elsewhere, Keith. If anyone will have you. But I'm not sure there's a big job market for dinosaur DJs over the age of sixty."

"We'll see. So who have you got lined up to do the breakfast show?"

"Ed Cowell."

"Hahaha, good luck with that! You know what they call him, don't you?"

"What?"

"The wokest man in Britain! What do you think my audience is going to make of that? They'll be switching off in droves."

"Which is exactly what we want. We're going to attract a new, more enlightened audience. Your current listeners are about as welcome here as you are. Speaking of which, it's time you were leaving. Are you going to go nicely, or shall I get Barry to throw you out?"

"I'm going, but there's nothing nice about it," said Keith, who was doing his best not to reveal how incandescent with rage he felt inside. "But I'll tell you one thing for nothing. You haven't seen the last of me."

"Oh, I think I have," said Nathalie. "And just think, it could all have been so different. If only you'd treated me differently all those years ago. Karma's a bitch, isn't it?"

"There's only one bitch in this room and it ain't karma," said Keith, making his way to the door and slamming it behind him.

He was acutely aware as he made the short walk to the lift that everyone in the open-plan office was staring at him. It was obvious that they all knew already. The victim was always the last to find out in these situations. He should know. He had seen plenty of others take this walk of shame over the years. It was the modern-day equivalent of walking the plank, and now it was his turn.

The only tiny consolation was that Barry, the most sarcastic security guard in the world, was not on reception when he called the lift. Perhaps he was busy escorting some other poor sod off the premises. He couldn't imagine many of the station's current line-up of presenters would be surviving this cull.

Outside, he emerged into the clear, cold winter air, wondering what to do next. Or rather, where to go next. His default option for so many years, whenever there was anything to celebrate or commiserate, was the same: the pub.

But which one? It wasn't like there were that many to choose from, not that he would consider worth going to these days, anyway. So many he used to like had closed down or been taken over and had the soul ripped out of them by pub companies refurbishing and rebranding them. Which, in his experience, was always for the worst.

The building in Canary Wharf he had just vacated for the last time was some way from his old haunts in Fleet Street. The conversation with Nathalie about those days had made him nostalgic for those boozy pubs, filled with proper old-school journalists, not the lame ducks the papers employed these days. But now, with all the good pubs gone and lunchtime drinking practically extinct, the only way to recreate that experience would be to travel back in time. It was something he had fantasised about many times but that's all it was, a fantasy. Everyone knew that time travel was just a plot device for films and books.

17

There was a pub close to the office where he might bump into some colleagues. Most of them used it for a lunch of the non-liquid variety now and again but he couldn't face running into them today. If they knew of his departure there would be sympathy and that was something he couldn't stand. The conversation would be awkward and he would feel uncomfortable. So, perhaps it would be better to go a little further afield.

In the end, he decided to take the underground to Soho, his favourite part of London. He would have a few drinks, grab a cheap Chinese buffet, and then have a few more drinks. Then, if he hadn't keeled over by midnight he would watch the mayor's woke firework display before going home to bed. He could leave worrying about what he was going to do for a living in the future until tomorrow.

Despite his high profile on the radio, he was still able to remain relatively incognito on the Tube because his voice was much better known than his face. Even so, he was far more grateful than usual when a passenger on the Jubilee Line recognised him and commended him on what a great show he had put on that morning. He didn't have the heart to tell the eager young man that it had been his last one.

He got off at Bond Street and walked the short distance to Soho, one of the few parts of London where he still felt at home. He had a destination in mind, a famous old pub where many legendary drinkers had held court over the years. Perhaps he would bump into a familiar face he hadn't seen for a while who wouldn't know of his loss of livelihood yet. He could cope with that. Or maybe a stranger he could put the world to rights with. That was the wonderful thing about pubs, or at least it used to be. You could meet anyone and anything could happen. He had met almost all of his past sexual partners whilst out drinking. Keith had never understood the point of the current fad for dating apps. Where was the spontaneity? The chemistry? It all seemed so contrived.

Considering the popularity of the venue, it was surprisingly quiet. Perhaps that was because it was New Year's Eve. People were saving themselves for the evening. Those that were there seemed to be mostly drinking soft drinks or lighter alcoholic drinks such as spritzers. There was barely a beer in sight and certainly no spirits. It was a far cry from the days in which he had first come into this pub when it had attracted every alcoholic in the neighbourhood.

Keith hadn't been in for a while. He had heard it had been taken over a few years ago by one of the main London breweries, which was confirmed by the sign outside and their name on the beer pumps. He remembered someone telling him that it had also gone vegan a while back but that didn't bother him, even though vegans were often the butt of his jokes on the show. He wasn't there to eat. That wasn't what pubs were for, in his opinion, though most companies seemed to think otherwise these days. The only thing on his agenda today was whisky, lots of it, and he was pretty sure that almost all alcohol was vegan by default.

No one seemed to recognise him, which was something that dwelt on his mind as he ordered his Scotch and made his way to a small table next to a piano, on a black-and-white mosaic floor. In the past, he would have been quite content in this scenario. He had never relished the prospect of being pestered by enthusiastic fans all the time. Now that it seemed fame was about to disappear, it was different. He needed any ego boost he could get, such as when that chap had approached him on the Tube.

Despite his intention to put the day's events out of his mind, as he sat alone with his Scotch it inevitably began to play on his mind. If he fell out of the public eye, how long would it be until everybody had forgotten him? What was he going to do now the radio show was gone? He had already lost the three newspaper columns he used to write over the past couple of years because his employers considered him too hot to handle. There was nothing to fall back on other than the podcast, and that only made peanuts. A previously annoying fan coming in now, singing his praises, and offering him drinks would give him a little encouragement. But none were forthcoming.

He sat pondering, with a glum expression on his face for a while, until the door to the right of him opened and a woman about his age entered the pub. With hair neatly coifed in a silver bun, she stepped inside in a thick woollen coat which provided plenty of protection against the December chill. Her matching knee-length skirt, in a shade of beige favoured by people over a certain age, didn't scream excitement, and neither did her old-fashioned brown tights. To Keith's eyes, she looked more like a librarian than the average lunchtime pub-goer.

It was obvious that she had never been in here before as she was looking around the room through her thick glasses as if trying to get her bearings. Curiously, he noticed she was glancing at her left wrist as if looking at a watch but there was nothing between the end of her coat sleeve and her hand.

Then she made a beeline for his table and, without even getting a drink first, sat down.

"I think you're the person I'm looking for," she said by way of introduction.

"Oh, really?" said Keith, taken aback by her unusual approach. A few years ago he would have responded with a chat-up line, but she hardly looked the type who would be open to offers, if he could even be bothered to try. Which he couldn't.

"Oh, yes, I was led here to find you."

"By whom?" asked Keith, intrigued. Unless the local Women's Institute was planning to ask him to judge their latest cake-making contest, he couldn't see what someone who looked like her could want with someone like him.

"Not by who," she said, keeping up the intrigue. "But by what."

She had piqued his interest, but he couldn't allow the conversation to continue without remembering his manners.

"Listen, Miss..."

"Haversham," she replied. "Elizabeth Haversham."

"Keith Diamond," he replied. "Now, before we go on, I wouldn't be a gentleman if I didn't offer you a drink."

"That's very generous of you, Keith. I'll have a sweet sherry."

"One sweet sherry coming up," said Keith, heading up to the bar and getting himself another double Scotch while he was at it. If put on the spot he could have correctly guessed her choice of drink. He prided himself on being able to identify a person's favourite tipple just by looking at them, and she had sherry written all over her.

It was a beverage that he rarely saw being drunk in pubs. Looking at her as he returned with the drinks, he had to wonder if she had ever been in a place like this before in her life. Luckily for her, it was quiet. What would she have made of the place in its heaving 1980s heyday?

"So, Miss Haversham, what brings you to this esteemed establishment? No offence, but this doesn't look like the sort of place you usually hang out."

"It isn't," she said. "Libraries are more my thing."

"I never would have guessed," said Keith. "So what could you possibly want with me, then? I'm not exactly well read. I don't think I've been in a library since primary school, and that was only when we were playing hide and seek at lunchtime. No one would ever have thought of looking for me there."

"I imagine not," said Elizabeth.

"But you've managed to find me. How exactly?"

"That's what I'm about to tell you. Your life is about to change for the better."

"I find that very hard to believe. I've just been sacked. Now come on, how did you find me?"

He leant forward eagerly, clasping his hands together in front of him and resting them beneath his chin, keen to hear what she had to say.

"With the help of this," she said, placing her hand on her wrist, where he had noticed her looking earlier.

"With what?" he asked. "There's nothing there."

"Oh, there is," she said, keeping the mystery going. "You just can't see it yet. Touch my wrist."

"That's very forward of you, Miss Haversham. We've only just met."

"Spare me your patter, Mr Diamond. I do know who you are, in case you were wondering."

"Really? You don't strike me as the average ChatFM listener."

"I have Twitter," she said.

"That would explain it," he replied, having trended many times on the platform, and rarely in a positive light.

"Go on, touch my wrist."

He did as she instructed, reaching forward tentatively, but before he reached her flesh, he hit something invisible and solid.

"I say, what's that?" he asked.

"You'll like this bit," she replied.

As Keith's fingers brushed against the invisible object on Elizabeth's wrist, an extraordinary transformation unfolded before his eyes. Out of nothingness, a solid gold bracelet shimmered into existence, adorning her wrist with a delicate, intricate design. Its centrepiece was an enchanting green jewel, glimmering with a radiance that suggested some sort of power source.

As he watched, the jewel pulsed, and then things got seriously weird. Under its own power, the bracelet seemed to come alive, detaching itself from Elizabeth and before he could react, wrapping itself around his arm like a snake. The green jewel blinked once, as if acknowledging the binding of two entities before the light faded and it looked just like a normal bracelet again.

But that was something it most certainly was not. It had a presence that he could feel. Whatever this thing was, it was alive and had just become part of him. Instinctively he reached to try to take it off, but it was fixed solid.

"What did you just do?" he gasped, wondering what strange sorcery this frumpy spinster had just bestowed upon him.

"I didn't do anything," replied Elizabeth. "The bracelet did. It chose me, and now it has chosen you."

"I don't want to be chosen by anything, thank you," said Keith. "I do the choosing about what happens in my life."

"Why don't I explain a little more about it before you jump to conclusions?" she replied.

"I think you better had," said Keith, an apprehensive look on his face at this peculiar turn of events.

"Right, well, it's like this. On New Year's Eve last year, I was in a coffee shop, reading a book, when a man came up to me and more or less performed the same trick on me that I've just pulled on you."

"So, you admit it's a trick, then?"

"Please, let me finish. He explained that he had just spent a year in 1978, guided by the bracelet, and now it was time to pass it on to me. He explained how it all worked, and then, on the stroke of midnight, I found myself in 1979 where I spent the whole of the next year."

"Come off it," said Keith sceptically. "This sounds like the sort of crap I used to make up when I worked for the *Sunday Sport*. You can't honestly expect me to swallow that?"

"Oh, it's true, and you'll find out soon enough. But I advise you to sit and listen because you're going to need to know how all this works when you go back to 1980."

"1980?" he replied, perking up at the thought. "I wouldn't mind going back to 1980 after the day I've had today."

"Perhaps that is why the bracelet chose you. It always chooses people for a reason. Some serious things happened in my life in 1979. My year there helped me confront them. Oh, and I had a lot of fun too."

"But why? What's the purpose of it all?"

"John, that's the name of the chap that gave the bracelet to me, explained that it's an ancient device that's been passed down from person to person for hundreds of years. Its purpose is to send whoever takes possession of it back in time forty years, so that they may maintain the timeline for a year. And that's what you are about to become. The new custodian of time."

"But why? I mean, why forty years? Why not twenty, or thirty?"

25

"No one knows. But it always chooses someone in our age group. Someone with plenty of life experience who was young then, and knows the future as it is supposed to be. John said that from time to time, events occur or things can go wrong that need to be put right. Or sometimes, it's just a case of keeping the train on the right track. Prevention is better than cure, as they say."

"Yes, but how do you know what things? I wouldn't know where to start."

"The bracelet tells you. It gets into your head. And it glows red or green to let you know if you're on the right path. Oh, and there are rules."

"What sort of rules?" replied Keith, his enthusiasm waning. "I don't like rules. And what if I meet myself?"

"You can't meet yourself because you'll be transported into your younger body. That's one of the real advantages."

"I'll say," said Keith, thinking of the possibilities. Young and fit again. That meant freedom. And not having to go to the toilet every twenty minutes, which incidentally he now needed to do again. And a decent sex life!

"I should point out that you are not there for personal gain. If you try and do things the bracelet doesn't approve of, it will let you know."

"Oh, great," said Keith, who was struggling to process all the ups and downs of this. One minute he felt excited at the idea but then the next thing she said left him deflated. "As if there isn't enough moralising in the present day, now I'm going to have this thing monitoring my every move in the past. So are you saying I can't do anything to improve my lot?"

"It depends on what you're talking about. If you're thinking of spending the whole time in the betting shop to try and make a fortune, don't. It's been tried and it doesn't work. But if you can do things to make you a better person or improve the lives of others around you then the bracelet will probably approve."

"After the day I've had, I don't want to be a better person. In fact, I want to be a worse person. I'm so pissed off with the world right now that I want to be the worst person I can possibly be."

"Now, you don't mean that, Keith, you're just lashing out at the world because things haven't been going right for you lately. Let me assure you, this is a chance to turn things around."

"I thought you said I couldn't change the timeline, so how can I improve my life, or anyone else's come to that, without screwing it up? That is how this sort of thing works, isn't it? What was that film a few years ago? *The Butterfly Effect*?"

"It's not as clear-cut as that. Every scenario you come up against will require a different approach. Sometimes you're changing things, other times you are preventing things from being changed."

"I'm sorry, that's too vague. I can, but I can't, depending on the situation. Confuse me a bit more, why don't you?"

"It will all make sense when you get there. If the bracelet chose you it will have been with good reason and it will guide you. Don't worry, I was confused too but you'll get the hang of it, and think of the benefits. At the very least, you are getting the chance to live a whole year of your life over again when you were young. Who wouldn't jump at the chance of such an opportunity!"

"Good point," said Keith, who was surprised that he was accepting this woman's story so easily, but maybe that was the influence of the bracelet. He could feel the power emanating from it, which had removed a large degree of his scepticism.

Then another thought struck him.

"Is it dangerous?" he asked. "I mean, what happens if I die?"

"I don't know," she said. "I did get into a couple of scrapes but came out unscathed. Somehow, I always felt that the bracelet was protecting me."

"And what happens when the year's up?"

"You come back. I've already been back a year. You don't miss any time here. You keep the bracelet for that year and then pass it on to someone else on the next New Year's Eve. Like I just have."

"How do I know who to pass it on to?"

"The bracelet will lead you to them. That's how I came to be here today."

"What if I lose the bracelet?"

"You can't. It's attached to you. And no one can steal it, either, because no one else can see it. I can't see it anymore. Only you can."

"OK, good. Is that it?"

"That's it."

"When do I depart?"

"On the stroke of midnight."

"Good. At least I won't have to endure that bloody firework display."

"Great," said Elizabeth. "Well, I must go. Good luck, Keith, and make the most of it. It truly is the most amazing experience."

"I'll say," he replied as she got up, leaving him nursing his whisky.

As soon as she was out of the door, he made a beeline for the gents. He had been dying to go for the past ten minutes but didn't want to admit in front of her that he needed to go. Thankfully, he wouldn't have that problem anymore when he made it back to 1980.

He glanced at his watch on his right wrist as he washed his hands, to see it had just gone two. He was impatient to get started, and ten hours seemed an awful long time to wait.

As for the bracelet on the other wrist, that seemed to have gone dormant for now and he could no longer sense any power emanating from it. It would probably wake up again after he had travelled back in time, assuming this was all real. It was outlandish and crazy but Elizabeth had been very convincing. And he couldn't deny the reality of the bracelet's existence.

He got another drink and returned to his table to contemplate the adventure that lay ahead.

What was it going to be like?

What was he going to do?

Elizabeth was right – this was an amazing opportunity and he couldn't wait for it to begin.

January 1980

"Keith, you bastard!"

Jimmy's exclamation echoed through the lively crowd, drowned out by the collective chorus of "Happy New Year!" from revellers all around.

In the blink of an eye, Keith found himself amidst a sea of people, right in front of a fountain in Trafalgar Square. It was precisely where, on the stroke of midnight, he had pulled a prank on Jimmy, sending his friend tumbling into the water.

That moment had slipped from Keith's memory until now. Sharing a flat with Jimmy in his younger years had bred a familiarity, sometimes on the fringe of contempt, that often led to those sorts of antics. Dunking him in the fountain was just one in a long line of similar pranks.

He looked around, marvelling at the sights. Everything Elizabeth had told him was true. He was forty years in the past when Trafalgar Square used to be the focus of the New Year celebrations. The area around the fountains was bustling with thousands of people in a partying mood, their breath forming frosty clouds in the frigid night air. Men and women, young and old, had gathered to usher in the new decade, and the thing that caught Keith's eye right away was the amazing range of fashions on display.

Many of the women were dressed in long coats with oversized collars, some fur-trimmed, and many belted tightly at the waist to create an hourglass silhouette. Others were clad in chunky-knit sweaters in bold colours like mustard yellow, pine green, and deep burgundy.

Their legs were encased in thick, patterned tights, and many wore knee-high leather boots which Keith recalled had been popularised by Debbie Harry, of Blondie fame. Of those who wore jeans, he was surprised to see that there were still a lot of flares on display, which he found surprising. He thought they had gone out by the end of the decade, but it seemed they were still lingering on. Most notable of all was the amount of hair – with big, bushy perms being the order of the day.

His first impression was that he had arrived in the 1970s rather than the 1980s, because the looks of both the women and the men were reminiscent of that earlier decade but then perhaps that was to be expected. He was on the cusp of the two eras, and seventies fashions would doubtless spill over into the new decade for a while yet.

The long hair was also prevalent on the men, many of whom were still sporting the long, shaggy styles of the 1970s. Some wore tailored suits with wide lapels and as for their shirts, they had bold patterns and large collars. He even spotted a kipper tie on one guy who looked like he had come fresh from presenting a class for the Open University on BBC2.

Others were less formally dressed, embracing the punk rock style with leather jackets adorned with studs and badges. Also, in stark contrast to the long hair of the majority, there were several skinheads on display. The most striking thing about the whole scene was how much diversity of fashion there was and how much effort people had put into defining themselves through their appearance. It was a far cry from the future where few people could be arsed to make an effort anymore and were content to wander around in cheap T-shirts and joggers from Sports Direct or Primark, faces glued to their phones.

The atmosphere in Trafalgar Square was a lively mix of excitement and anticipation for the new decade. People were huddled together, laughing, and sharing drinks from hip flasks. The strains of a punk rock anthem from the band Generation X could be heard from a portable ghetto blaster, and the scent of cigarette smoke filled the air. Looking around, Keith was amazed at how many people were smoking. He had smoked himself in this era. How was that going to work? Would he be craving one now he was back in his old body?

As Jimmy clambered back out of the fountain, Keith couldn't help but marvel at how young his lifelong friend looked, which in turn led him to contemplate his own appearance.

Although he couldn't see his face, Keith knew that in his youth he had possessed a full head of curly black locks. He left these untamed to grow as they pleased, lending him a wild, tousled quality that perfectly complemented his charming persona. He looked down at his clothing, recognising his old black leather jacket, personalised with an array of sewn-on badges. These proudly showcased his punk rock rebellion phase during his university days, which although he now had a full-time job, he wasn't ready to shake off. Beneath the jacket, he wore a T-shirt featuring his favourite band, The Clash. His lean frame and confident posture had made him a young man who had the world at his feet.

What had gone wrong? How had he descended from this youthful version of himself to the middle-aged lump he had become later in life? Was it just the inevitable ravages of time, or should he have looked after himself better? If he had swapped all those boozy nights out and kebabs for the gym and a healthy diet, might he have been able to keep himself trim? Undoubtedly, it would have made a difference but he wouldn't have had as much fun along the way.

Jimmy was also not as big in this era, in comparison to his older self, when he was even larger than Keith. Yet back in these times, he had already been carrying a decent amount of weight. By 2019 standards, no one would have labelled this version of Jimmy as fat, but the population in the future was much heavier than it was now. Hence, in this environment, Jimmy's moderately chubby frame stood out in a crowd that on average was remarkably lean.

As for the rest of his appearance, Jimmy wasn't as fashionable as Keith. He wore a cheap ill-fitting cream suit from Burton, sodden from his unexpected dip in the fountain. On top of his head was a matted mop of mousy hair, sopping wet from being submerged. All in all, it did not add up to a very flattering appearance.

Even at the best of times, he gave off a downtrodden aura in comparison to Keith's sharp and charismatic persona. It was obvious to everyone who encountered them who was the alpha male of the two.

"I'm completely bloody soaked now," complained Jimmy. "And absolutely freezing to boot. I'm going to have to go home and change."

"Sorry about that," said Keith with complete insincerity, chuckling at Jimmy's dishevelled appearance. He had performed the dunking just a split second before he had taken possession of this body, and already he was beginning to see that being back here in the past had the potential to be a lot of fun.

"Yeah, of course you are," said Jimmy. "And on my birthday too. I'll get you back for this, see if I don't. Now, come on, let's go."

"What, not joining in with *Auld Lang Syne*?" asked Keith, as strangers all around began to link hands and sing.

"No, I'm not in the mood. You've ruined it, as usual. I want to go home."

Home, mused Keith. Where was home? It was going to be quite a challenge adapting to his life from forty years before. How much would he remember?

He had many memories of sharing a flat with Jimmy. Several flats. They tended to be on the move quite often back then, from one shithole to another. Which one were they in right now? Never mind, he would just have to follow Jimmy and find out.

As they made their way through the crowds, he caught the eye of a couple of girls dressed up in sexy Santa outfits who smiled back at him, sending his imagination into overdrive. This was amazing. He was young again. He was fit. Women fancied him again and he intended to make the most of it. Sod the bracelet and its prissy rules. Why not just make the most of the opportunity and spend the entire year shagging?

As soon as this thought went through his head, he felt a pulse in his wrist and saw the bracelet glow red briefly, as if voicing its disapproval.

"Oh, I see," he said. "It's going to be like that, is it? Who are you, my moral compass?"

35

Just as he had suspected during his conversation with Elizabeth, the damned thing was trying to tell him what he should or shouldn't be doing. And no one told the Diamond Geezer what to do! He could see his relationship with the bracelet might very well be a fraught one.

"What are you talking about?" said Jimmy, assuming Keith had been addressing him.

"Oh nothing," he said, looking around for something he could use by way of explanation and focusing on a poster that made his blood run cold, on the side of a bus shelter up ahead. It was a large poster of Radio One DJ Jimmy Savile, accompanied by the slogan 'Clunk Click Every Trip'.

"Just that poster," said Keith. "Absolutely disgusting."

"Why? You may want to die crashing through a car windscreen, but I don't."

"That's not what I mean," said Keith, thinking about Savile's vile crimes for which he had never been punished. Should he mention it to his namesake, the other Jimmy? He decided for now that he would not but it threw up some interesting possibilities. Could he do anything about Savile while he was here? He looked down to the jewel on the bracelet for approval but it did not light up. It seemed it didn't have an opinion on this one.

"I need a cigarette," said Jimmy, reaching inside the pocket of his sodden suit and pulling out a packet of Silk Cut. But when he flipped open the top he was dismayed to discover they were soaked through.

"Bloody hell, look what you've done," said Jimmy. "I'll have to have one of yours."

Keith reached inside his jacket pocket and pulled out a packet of Marlboro Red. As he did, by coincidence he looked up and saw a large billboard up ahead featuring the legendary Marlboro Man poster. Now, that was some advertising campaign. They didn't make them like that anymore.

The advert depicted a rugged cowboy in a picturesque Western setting. He was on horseback, complete with Stetson, denim jeans, leather chaps, and a weathered brown leather jacket. He was riding through an open prairie, with rolling hills, a bright blue sky, and a setting sun in the background. It looked idyllic.

The cowboy had a strong, stoic expression, suggesting masculinity, independence, and a carefree way of life. He was holding a cigarette in one hand, with a relaxed, confident demeanour. The message was clear: smoke Marlboro cigarettes and you can be like this guy!

How the world had changed. Such advertising was long banned in the twenty-first century, and not just for health reasons. A poster like this would not be deemed acceptable for any product, reeking as it did of what had become known as toxic masculinity. As for the attractive red and white cigarette packaging, which Keith recalled had adorned the cars of the McLaren Formula One team for many years, they had been replaced by pictures of blackened, diseased lungs from dying cancer patients.

Was it for the greater good, or state overreach? Keith wasn't sure, but the poster brought back happy memories as well as making him fancy a smoke. So the advertising was working. Maybe it was the Marlboro Man that had

37

led him to choose it as his preferred brand in the first place. But he had given up the habit over a decade ago after the smoking ban had been introduced in pubs.

Should he smoke in this era? Would it make him want to smoke when he went back to his own time? He debated the possibilities. He wasn't supposed to be messing around with the timeline and since he had smoked in this time, perhaps it was his duty to do so again.

"Come on," said Jimmy, getting impatient as Keith walked along holding the pack as he contemplated his decision.

"Here you go," said Keith, opening the pack. "Hope it's not too strong for you!"

Among the many memories flooding back was that he used to tease Jimmy about smoking the milder Silk Cuts rather than the more potent Marlboro.

"Aren't you having one?" asked Jimmy.

"Umm…no, said Keith, tentatively coming to a decision. "I'm thinking of giving them up. New Year's resolution."

As he said this, the jewel on the bracelet glowed green, showing its approval. This annoyed Keith. Bloody do-gooding thing. How dare it? It was time to show it who was the boss.

"That's not like you," said Jimmy.

"No, it's not, is it?" said Keith, reversing his decision and pulling out a cigarette. Instinctively he reached into his other pocket and pulled out a matching

Marlboro Zippo lighter, depicting the same man as the poster.

He lit Jimmy's, and then his own, watching with satisfaction, as the bracelet glowed red briefly before fading again. So what if it disapproved? It was hardly a pivotal decision that was going to affect the space-time continuum, was it? He could see that this new symbiotic relationship was going to take some getting used to and the device needed to understand that it couldn't dictate every tiny detail of how he lived his life.

He took a deep drag of the cigarette, initially savouring the rich, robust taste that filled his mouth. Then it hit the back of his throat like a searing fireball, causing him to cough heavily.

"Looks like you're the one who can't handle it!" said Jimmy, delighted at his discomfort.

It had certainly taken Keith by surprise, being much stronger than he had expected. Then he remembered that he had switched to smoking Marlboro Lights in later years. But he wouldn't be able to do that now, as he was pretty sure they hadn't come onto the market yet. When had they been launched? He had no idea and it was hardly as if he could go back to the future and Google to find out. There was no internet here. He was going to have to reacquaint himself with the old ways of finding things out, especially as being a journalist, it was part of his job.

Clueless as to where they were going or how they were going to get there, Keith let Jimmy lead the way. As they passed a row of shops, their neon signs casting colourful reflections on the wet pavement, he felt full of nostalgia seeing high street names that had long since disappeared. He would have to come and check these out, especially Tandy, an electronics shop he had loved tinkering about in. He couldn't remember when they had disappeared but the retail landscape was poorer without them.

The streets were still bustling with people, giving the city a vibrant feel even in these early hours of the morning. It was exactly how he remembered the London of his youth and he had heard it referred to many times as the city that never sleeps. Then again, he had heard that phrase bandied around regarding Paris and New York as well. Tonight it would be true of most major cities in the world, as their residents celebrated the arrival of another year.

They rounded a corner and reached a row of bus stops, where Jimmy abruptly stopped, holding out his hand to hail a red double-decker bus marked Whitechapel. The diesel engine grumbled as it came to a stop, and as they boarded at the rear, the conductor greeted them with his ticket machine at the ready.

For the first time since he had arrived, Keith needed to dig into his pockets for some money and noticed a change he had forgotten all about. His silver coins seemed massive compared to the twenty-first-century versions. One of them was so old it still had the head of George VI on it. Looking at it closely, he could see that it was an old shilling from 1948, which doubled up as a five-pence piece in the new currency.

The bus was almost full downstairs, and Jimmy made a beeline straight for the stairs.

"Come on, let's go up here, then we can smoke!" he exclaimed.

Smoking on buses, thought Keith, not relishing the prospect, especially following his recent fiery re-acquaintance with the habit. It was more his clothes he was concerned about and when he got up there he had every reason to be worried. The top deck was lined with layers of smoke as practically everyone aboard puffed away. There was a lively atmosphere with many inebriated passengers indulging in an impromptu singalong of 'Yellow Submarine'.

Keith and Jimmy grabbed the only double seat left near the front of the bus, parking themselves on worn-out red leather seats that squeaked when they sat down. The windows were smeared with raindrops and dirt, and Keith looked out as they passed more shops, including a branch of Our Price which had albums by The Police, Rod Stewart, and Abba in the window. He wasn't into any of those artists but even so, was looking forward to getting back into the music of the era. What was number one, he wondered? He would have to listen in to the Top 40 on Radio One when Sunday came around. He didn't yet know when that would be. It might have been New Year's Day but he had no idea what day of the week it had fallen on.

His musings were disturbed as the good-humoured atmosphere on the bus came to an abrupt halt. A couple of teenage lads about three seats behind them were devouring a box of Kentucky Fried Chicken and one of them obnoxiously decided to start chucking the bones over his shoulder as if he was a medieval king.

This did not go down well with a couple of skinheads sitting a few rows back, one of whom was struck on the head by a greasy drumstick, causing a small gash.

"What the fuck do you think you're playing at, mate?" called out the injured party, immediately jumping up and running up the bus to thump the culprit. Unfortunately, being somewhat inebriated, he picked out the wrong person and very quickly the conflict spread like wildfire as half the top deck decided to get involved.

This sort of kerfuffle had been commonplace in the 1980s, and Keith looked back with fascination as the aggravation played out behind him. As he did, the bracelet glowed red. What was it telling him? Did it expect him to intervene? For what purpose, to get his head kicked in? No thanks.

In the end it was all over quite quickly, with a couple of black eyes, and a few bruised egos before everyone returned to their seats.

"Better than staying in watching the telly, eh?" said Jimmy who had been enjoying the show too, relieved that the altercation hadn't reached their seats.

Keith didn't say anything but thought about how times had changed. Something like this wouldn't have been resolved so easily in his time. There was no such thing as a good old-fashioned punch-up anymore. If something like this had happened in 2019, the lad throwing the chicken would have stood a good chance of being stabbed to death, never mind a black eye. Knife crime had become rife in the capital and nobody seemed to be doing anything about it. It had been discussed on his radio show many times.

He still didn't know exactly where they were going. He remembered that they had lived in two vastly contrasting flats in Whitechapel, one of which they had dubbed the nice flat, and the other, the horrible flat. When Jimmy rang the bell on the bus and got up, indicating it was time to leave, they disembarked the bus outside a small row of shops in a dingy precinct, strewn with litter. With a sigh, Keith realised it was the horrible flat.

It was upstairs accommodation above an independent grocery store but there was no way in through the front door as the landlord, also the proprietor of the shop, had refused access that way. He didn't trust his tenants not to steal anything. Instead, they had to climb a clunky metal staircase behind the building that amounted to little more than a fire escape.

The doorway at the top led to a small landing, with a flat on either side. It was musty with a noticeable smell of damp and poorly lit even in the daytime, with the only light coming in through a small grimy window above the door, barely the width of a shoebox. At this time of night, it was almost pitch dark.

"Have you got your key?" asked Jimmy. "I think I forgot mine."

"Umm, I don't know," replied Keith, trying various pockets before to his relief locating a small copper Yale key. Memories of this flat were already coming back to him as he fumbled in the darkness for the keyhole and when he finally got the door open and found the light switch, it provided the hideous confirmation that it truly was as bad as he remembered.

The door led straight into the kitchen which was lit by a long overhead fluorescent tube that hummed and crackled as it warmed up to illuminate their truly humble abode.

The interior of their flat could only be described as chaotic. There was a pile of dirty dishes piled up in the cracked porcelain sink, and remnants of the previous evening's takeaway spread across the breakfast bar that was the closest thing they had to a dining table. They never used it, preferring to sit on the sofa when they ate. There was a grimy fridge in the corner that Keith didn't even dare to open, fearing what horrors might lie within, and a horrible smell pervading the whole area. This could only be coming from the brown plastic flip-top bin in the corner which didn't even appear to have a liner in it.

The living room, such as it was, was equally unkempt with more takeaway boxes on the floor along with empty beer bottles. A large part of the floor space was taken up by the truly hideous corner sofa, the well-worn fabric consisting of a gaudy pattern of different shades of orange, green and brown. In addition, there were several random splodges. Keith wasn't sure if they were part of the pattern or suspicious stains from God knows what. In front of it was a small coffee table which Keith thought was made of wood but since every inch of the surface was covered with mess it was hard to tell.

The sofa faced an old bulky television set, of a type which was a mainstay of 1970s and early 1980s living rooms. It stood precariously on a rickety wooden stand, its faux woodgrain finish surrounding the slightly curved glass screen which was standard for televisions of the time. It had six buttons on the front, though if Keith recalled correctly, there had only been three television channels at this time. Perhaps the manufacturers had been preparing for the future when the UK would have multichannel television, just like America, but that future was still a good decade away.

To cover up the patches of damp on the walls they had put up posters of various punk bands, including the classic cover from The Sex Pistols' *Never Mind the Bollocks* album. Another wall was covered by a large Union Jack flag which Keith recalled they had put there to cover a hole that a previous occupant had drilled through to the bathroom on the other side for reasons they didn't even want to think about.

The most interesting items were a battered record player and a pile of LPs and 7-inch singles beneath, which Keith immediately went to check out. He was curious to see what they had most recently been listening to and was pleased to see side A of the Madness album *One Step Beyond* on the turntable. He immediately switched the player on and placed the needle on the record.

"What are you doing?" said Jimmy crossly, as the opening monologue of the title track began booming out. "You remember what Mr McGregor said. No music after midnight. He said he would kick us out if we did it again."

"He'd be doing us a favour," said Keith. "I mean, look at this place."

"Yeah, and why did we end up here in the first place?" replied Jimmy, elbowing his way past Keith and turning the volume right down.

"I can't remember," said Keith, and he genuinely couldn't.

"Yes, you can. Our old landlord threw us out because you shagged his daughter."

"Ah, yeah!" said Keith, a pleasant memory flooding back. So that was why they had left the nice flat.

"Right, so let's not have a repetition," said Jimmy, switching off the player.

"Might as well go to bed then," said Keith, who suddenly felt extremely fatigued. It had been a long day – or two days, depending on how he looked at it.

Unfortunately, he had forgotten the layout of the flat and chose the wrong bedroom door. He realised his mistake as soon as he opened it and flicked on the light switch, to be confronted by more flesh than you would find on a nudist beach.

Every inch of every wall was covered with pictures of naked women. Some were black and white newspaper clippings from the tabloids, including the one they worked for. Others were more intimate colourful spreads from the magazines that could be found on the top shelves of every newsagent in the country. For the second time that night, Keith's attention was caught by the amount of hair on the women, though this time it wasn't just up top. Fashions had changed in a lot of areas.

"Oi, what's your game?" protested Jimmy. "That's my bedroom!"

"Don't you mean your wanking emporium? I mean, seriously, Jimmy, this is a bit pervy, don't you think?"

"You know I've got my heart set on a career in glamour photography. I'm fed up with taking pictures at football matches and boring royal events. All this stuff is just for research purposes."

"Yeah, that's what they all say," replied Keith. "But look, have you considered what's going to happen in the unlikely event you ever manage to persuade a real woman to come back here? What's she going to think if she comes into your bedroom and sees all this lot?"

"I'll take them down first."

"Really, and how long's that going to take? I mean, what are they stuck on with? No, don't answer that, I don't want to know."

"Look, just get out of my room," said Jimmy, annoyed.

"Don't worry, I will," said Keith, trying the other door and to his relief finding the sanctuary of his own room. It was much cooler than Jimmy's, with walls covered with more punk album covers and movie posters, including one from *Diamonds Are Forever*. He enjoyed collecting anything cool that had his surname in the title.

He was exhausted and flopped down onto the bed, falling asleep almost straightaway. The next thing he heard was Jimmy banging on the door.

"Come on, Keith! We're going to be late for the match!"

He sat up and looked around. It was daylight but there was no clock in the room. He glanced at the bracelet but it was inert. No saving the world needed this morning then. If it even was still morning.

47

What match was Jimmy talking about? He had no idea but it was probably work-related. The pair of them had begun working at the newspaper the previous autumn and were very much at the bottom of the journalistic pile. They never got anywhere near any juicy stories, and a large part of their job was going to cover football matches. It wasn't particularly glamorous but they got in for free, which was of more interest to Jimmy than it was to him. Keith wasn't particularly interested in football unless it was an England game, though in later years he had pretended to support West Ham to bolster his fake East End credentials.

He got up, desperate for the loo, having not yet been since his arrival in 1980. What a wonderful thing it was to have such a strong bladder. He was going to enjoy the next year of not having to be constantly worrying about his next toilet visit.

However, this morning's visit was not enjoyable in any shape or form. If he thought the kitchen had been bad, the filth in the bathroom was off the scale. He couldn't live like this. It had been fine forty years ago but he had grown used to less squalid surroundings in the interim, and this disgusting flat was one aspect of his younger life that was best left in the past.

"We need to get out of that flat," he said to Jimmy, on the train, on their way to Selhurst Park where the delights of Crystal Palace vs Norwich City awaited them. He was racking his brains trying to remember where they had gone to live next. Was it the place in Bethnal Green? That hadn't been so bad, unlike his memory. It was shocking how much he had forgotten.

"We signed a twelve-month lease in November," said Jimmy.

"Bloody hell. Right, well we need to clean up then. A proper rota. It's proper minging in there."

"Since when has that ever bothered you? A couple of nights ago you were revelling in it, saying that even though we had jobs now we were still going to live the rock 'n' roll lifestyle."

"Yeah, well maybe I've grown up a bit since then."

"In two days?"

"It feels like a lot longer," said Keith, wondering whether he should tell Jimmy about the strange turn of events that had brought him here. He decided not to bother for the moment. Perhaps later once he had settled in, if it became necessary for some reason.

It was lively on the way into the stadium, with a few fans spinning old-fashioned rattles around, creating a harsh clacking sound. Keith stopped to buy a programme from a street seller wearing a red and blue Crystal Palace scarf. It was only 20p so he sifted through his pockets and handed over a couple of chunky ten-pence pieces. He didn't have any twenty-pence coins, perhaps they hadn't been introduced yet. What did and didn't exist in 1980? It was hard to recall. Still, whatever the available coinage was, he loved how cheap everything was. He couldn't wait to go for a pint and get change from a pound note. Or maybe even a fifty-pence piece. How much was a pint? He would hazard a guess at about 50p.

He had to get directions to the press office at the ground as like almost everywhere he had been so far, he couldn't remember the way. He and Jimmy had parted company by this time with his flatmate going down to a prime spot by the pitch. There he would be trying to get the perfect snap of a centre forward firing home a perfectly timed shot into the back of the net, in the hope that it would make the back page of tomorrow's paper.

No such luck. It was one of the most boring matches Keith had ever seen, and he struggled to write things down on the scraps of paper he had scrounged off the other journalists, having neglected to bring a notepad with him. He was going to have to work hard to adjust to his old life as he had forgotten so much of what he used to do. If it hadn't been for Jimmy, he wouldn't have even known he was supposed to have come here, which would probably have meant a serious dressing-down at work. He couldn't risk losing his job. Much as he took the piss out of his flatmate, he realised he was going to be leaning on him very heavily to get through these first few days.

"Bloody nil-nil!" complained Jimmy, as they made their way out of the stadium along with a somewhat subdued crowd. Often there were fights after the games but not today.

"I didn't get one decent photo," he added. "So there's no chance of me getting anything in tomorrow's edition. It hardly seems worth bothering to go back to the office. Shall we go and get a pint instead? It's nearly opening time. And it's my birthday, remember? Twenty-two today!"

Opening time! Another blast from the past. Of course, pubs still shut in the afternoon. Keith struggled to remember what time they reopened. Half five, perhaps.

"Oh, I still think we should go in, I've got to write the match report," said Keith, more confident that he knew where to go this time but keen to keep Jimmy by his side just in case. Although he was still very much finding his bearings, he had been to his former place of employment hundreds of times and the route was ingrained in his mind.

"That won't take long," said Jimmy. "This isn't a game that's going to live long in the memory."

"You don't know how right you are," said Keith, who had zero recollection of watching this game the first time he had presumably attended it, forty years before. "Now, let's get back to the newsroom."

The office building on Fleet Street that served as the HQ of the newspaper in the 1980s was an imposing structure, with a grand entrance composed of large glass doors flanked by stone columns. Above the doors, a sign bearing the newspaper's name in bold red neon shone as a bright beacon in the early evening darkness. It was one of many newspapers based on the street at this time and the area was bustling with reporters, heading back to file their reports for the following day's editions.

Upon entering the newsroom, Keith was met with waves of activity, noise, and smoke. It was a large open space with rows of desks containing typewriters at which journalists were typing furiously. He recognised a lot of familiar faces, many of whom he now knew were long dead, either from old age or from the ravages of a lifestyle dependent on cigarettes and alcohol. There were stacks of newspapers, files, and reference books scattered around, and the walls were adorned with framed copies of some of the paper's most famous front

51

pages, along with a collection of Page 3 girls proudly displaying their assets.

Keith thought back to what Nathalie had said about her time here and had to admit, she might have had a point. As he thought this, the bracelet briefly glowed green to show it agreed, which again annoyed him. It was treating him like a small child with a reward chart and it made him think about the Thought Police from Orwell's *1984*. But even they had not been able to physically read minds like this thing could. It was a truly intrusive form of surveillance and that was something he had always railed against. Unless, of course, the surveillance was being performed by him in the pursuit of a juicy story. Then it was fine as it was in the public interest.

To say the room was lively would have been putting it mildly. It was a cacophony of ringing telephones, clattering typewriters and people jumping up with their copy and rushing to the back of the room to submit their work to the editors. All of this took place against a background hum of conversation as the different teams discussed the stories and made decisions about what would make the first editions. This included a lot of banter and piss-taking. It was what got them through the days, along with tobacco and alcohol.

Despite the length of time that had passed since Keith last entered this room, he still remembered where his desk was and made his way over to it, getting involved in the inevitable banter on the way.

"Alright, Keith, ya twat," said a particularly gobby journalist by the name of Gordon as he passed his desk. He was about ten years older than him and wrote for the paper's entertainment section under several alter egos.

One of these involved pretending to be an astrologer to write the horoscopes, and another was an agony aunt for the problem page which was basically just an excuse to publish smutty stories.

"Wanker," said Bob, the paper's chief photographer. This was what life had been like in the old office. The atmosphere could be hostile, yet Keith drew a strange comfort from it. This was very early in his career, and being low in the pecking order he was an obvious target for the older journalists to pick on. But all that would soon change. Within a few years, he would be the top dog in this newsroom.

He sat down at his desk next to an ageing journalist called Ted, who had been around so long he had started out working as a war correspondent for *The Times* in the 1940s. He had been one of the more affable people in the room, having mellowed with age by the 1980s. During Keith's first year, Ted had given him some invaluable advice to help him forge his fledgling career. He was also very generous with the bottle of Scotch that he kept in his desk drawer to keep them going on evenings when they were running against the clock to get the paper out. Keith remembered being gutted when Ted died of cancer, only a few months after he retired.

Among the typewriters which predominated, he noticed a few of the old-style mainframe terminals that in 1980 were state of the art. These were beginning to revolutionise the way the newsroom operated during this period. Technology was in its infancy compared to what Keith was used to, and here he was, right back at the dawn of the information revolution. He noticed that the terminals were available only to some of the more senior journalists and editors. They featured bright green LED lettering on a dark background which hurt the eyes if you looked at it too long. Even above the general cacophony of the newsroom he could hear the buzz and feel the heat that the bulky things gave off.

He didn't have a terminal. He wasn't senior enough. Ted didn't have one either. He had been offered one but turned it down as he did not believe in such things. He was old school, through and through. So Keith sat down, pulled his crumpled notes out of his pocket, and tried to get to grips with the old typewriter. It was tough going, and he made plenty of mistakes. There was no backspace key or edit undo facility here, so he just pressed on with it, planning to apologise to the editor for the typos later. Once the editor had been over his report, it would go off to the typesetters who were highly skilled women who would get it ready for publication.

As he typed he overheard a conversation to the right of the room between Jimmy and Jerry, their boss, a former third-division goalkeeper who was now forging a new career as a functioning alcoholic in the world of journalism. He had managed to rise to the position of deputy editor largely due to the high rate of attrition in the office, i.e. people dying.

Jerry was very tall, a useful attribute for a goalkeeper. He was only in his forties but looked older, largely due to his adoption of the Bobby Charlton comb-over hairstyle favoured by bald blokes of the time. It did nothing for him. In addition, his dull grey suit looked like something he had inherited from his grandfather. But that was the way in this era. After a certain age, roughly thirty-five, it seemed almost everyone dressed like an old man. To complete the picture of middle age, he was smoking an old-fashioned pipe.

"So, in other words, you've come back with bugger all again, Jimmy," said Jerry.

"I defy even David Bailey to come away from that travesty of a game with any sort of decent shot," replied Jimmy.

"Well, since you've made no valid contribution whatsoever, you can compile the football results."

"Bloody hell, do I have to?"

"Yes and I'm afraid the Telex machine is on the blink so you'll have to get them off Ceefax," said Jerry, gesturing at a recently installed portable television set with a remote control that allowed access to the BBC's information service.

Keith watched, fascinated, as Jimmy struggled to get to grips with the primitive technology, desperately trying to write down the information before the page flipped over. It was one of the annoying things about the Teletext service over which the user had no control. But he had a certain fondness for it. In a way, it was like a very early forerunner of the internet. It also had the date and time on it which confirmed that today was a Tuesday.

Things were more fraught in the newsroom than usual, with various technical problems disrupting the evening's proceedings. But at last, the two of them found themselves back out on the street where they had only one destination in mind: the pub.

Discovering that a pint was just 47p, less than his earlier estimate, was most welcome. It was less than one-tenth of what he had been paying in 2019, and that, in addition to the vigour of his renewed youth and Jimmy's desire to celebrate his birthday, made for a lively night. When he awoke, even a minor hangover couldn't dampen his spirits. He had successfully navigated his way through his first day and now he had a whole year to play with.

February 1980

"This is boring," said Jimmy, as he and Keith sat on their garish sofa, cans of Hofmeister in hand, watching the antiquated television in the corner. "Turn it over."

A month had passed since Keith had arrived in 1980 and it was remarkable how quickly he had slipped back into his former life. Sure, the first few days had been a little tricky as he got to grips with things but by the end of the first week, it was as if the last forty years had never happened. He had managed to keep his secret from Jimmy too. Apart from the odd moment here or there when he hadn't been able to resist dropping hints about future events, he had not given anyone any reason to suspect him. Most of the time what he said just went straight over their heads.

This was a rare night in, especially considering that it was a Saturday, which was their day off as the paper they worked for wasn't published on a Sunday. The reason they had not gone out was that Jimmy was suffering from a terrible cold. With the fuss he was making over it, anyone would have thought he was about to keel over and die. His illness didn't stop Keith from going out on his own, but for once he didn't fancy it. The weather was lousy, with sleety, freezing rain falling across the capital, and besides, he could do with a night in. The past month had been extremely hectic.

He had been working six days a week and out nearly every night. During that time he had brought three women home with him. They had all been one-night stands but there was nothing untoward about it. All three had been single and in their early twenties, just like he now was, and the bracelet hadn't shown any disapproval. What was odd was that he couldn't remember any of these women from his previous life. He didn't think that he had merely forgotten about them but that it was more likely that he had not met any of them the first time around.

He had met all three on nights out when he knew that he could not have been following the exact pattern of behaviour he had before. How could he? There was no way he could remember the precise details of everything he had said and done and every place he had been on any given day for a whole year. No one would after forty years. So it was different places and different people, but did it really matter? His hook-ups were meaningless because none of the women expressed any desire to see him again. He wasn't sure why that was – perhaps they were put off by the manky state of his flat after spending the night there but it didn't matter. The last thing he wanted was a relationship when he was only here for the short term.

It did lead him to wonder about this whole process of coming back in time. Surely, just by being here, he was messing things up. He had never met those three women before. What consequences might come from what he had done with them? What if one of them got pregnant? He had used protection but even so, there were no guarantees. And what about all the other people he interacted with every day? All those encounters had the potential to alter things too.

But if the bracelet wasn't objecting, then presumably the things he was doing didn't matter. It didn't seem to want him to do very much at all. When he had first come back in time he had envisaged that he would be spending his time here living like some sort of superhero, righting wrongs, and saving the world every day. Instead, all he did was hang out with Jimmy either at work, in the flat, or the pub, guzzle copious amounts of booze, smoke endless cigarettes and chat up women at every opportunity. In other words, exactly what he had done when he had previously been this age. It was enjoyable but in terms of his supposed position as the custodian of time, rather underwhelming.

This evening was particularly uninspiring. Right now, he was sitting on the sofa drinking piss-weak lager, listening to Jimmy coughing his guts up, and watching some long-forgotten chat show hosted by Faith Brown on ITV.

The lack of a functional remote control meant that Keith had to get out of his seat to change the channel on the television. When he pressed the button to put it on to BBC1 he got the seal of approval from Jimmy, who made about the first cheery comment he had come out with all day.

"Ah, yes, that's better," said his flatmate, as comedy legend Dick Emery filled the screen. "I like him."

"Good, well at least we agree on something," said Keith, as he went to sit back down. They had been arguing over the television all day. With Jimmy being ill he had taken up residency on the sofa, and with the weather being so lousy, Keith hadn't fancied going out on his own. He could have gone to a football match but just wasn't interested enough in the game to make the effort. He wouldn't get in for free either. They didn't cover the Saturday fixtures as part of their job. That was the preserve of the journalists who worked for the Sunday papers.

In the morning, he had wanted to watch *Tiswas* but Jimmy had insisted on *Swap Shop* much to Keith's annoyance. To say he was not a fan of Noel Edmonds would have been an understatement. Eventually, he had agreed to settle the issue on the toss of a coin, which he had promptly lost. Jimmy wasn't interested in his offer of a best out of three so he had been forced to spend the morning watching the bearded wonder grinning at him out of the screen for about three hours.

On the plus side, part of the deal was that he got to choose what sport they watched in the afternoon. This involved flicking between Frank Bough presenting *Grandstand* on BBC1 and Dickie Davies hosting *World of Sport* on ITV.

Frank Bough – now there was a name to conjure with. He was one of a long line of supposedly respectable television presenters who had disgraced themselves in later years. Keith knew because he had been instrumental in breaking the scandalous revelations of the seemingly benign, middle-aged Bough's penchant for cocaine and prostitutes when it all came out in the late 1980s.

It wasn't even that scandalous by twenty-first-century standards, but back then, that sort of thing was still a big deal. Right now, Bough's downfall was still a long time away but Keith couldn't resist testing the water with Jimmy while they watched to see his reaction.

"See that fellow there? There's more to him than meets the eye, Jimmy. Drugs and hookers, that's what he's into."

"Don't be ridiculous. He's a total square! I mean look at him. He looks like some boring uncle that sits in the corner at family functions talking about his allotment."

"It'll all come out in time. You'll see."

And he had left it at that. After the sport, they enjoyed some *Pink Panther* cartoons, and then after that came the infamous *Jim'll Fix It*. Keith was sick to death of seeing that evil paedophile's face plastered all over the place, especially as it seemed the whole nation adored him. How could he have hoodwinked everybody for so long? He dropped a couple of hints about Savile during the programme but Jimmy seemed oblivious and he couldn't be bothered to explain further. He would save it for another day.

As Keith sat back down to enjoy Dick Emery, Jimmy had his most theatrical coughing fit yet. Grabbing a tissue, he blew his nose heavily and then tossed it onto an ever-growing pile on the table in front of him. At Keith's insistence, particularly after comments from the last woman he had brought back, the flat had been kept tidier than it had been when he had first seen it at New Year. A pile of snotty tissues all over the place he could do without.

"Do you have to do that?" exclaimed Keith. "It's disgusting! You're spreading your filthy germs everywhere."

"I can't help it," bleated Jimmy pathetically. "I'm not a well man."

"Go to bed, then, if you're that ill," said Keith, as the closing credits to *The Dick Emery Show* began to roll.

"If I go to bed, I'll feel worse," said Jimmy, draining the last of his lager and lighting up another ciggie.

"I hardly think that's going to help," said Keith, "Your lungs could do with a rest," aware of the hypocrisy of this statement, considering the packet of Marlboro and accompanying ashtray on the table in front of him.

"On the contrary," argued Jimmy. "Smoke's bad for you, right? They use fumigation to get rid of pests so it must be bad for viruses too. All those germs in my throat, well, this is my way of smoking them out. And the same goes for the alcohol though this crappy lager isn't cutting it. I reckon I need something stronger."

"I'm not surprised. It's only 3.2%. I told you to get Löwenbräu."

"I know, but I liked the advert for this one with the bear on the telly. Anyway, you know that film we saw the other night where that cowboy used bourbon to sterilise the wound after an arrow got him in the leg? Well, I need something like that to sterilise whatever's in my throat. Along with the smoke, the germs won't stand a chance."

"That's the worst theory I have ever heard," said Keith, looking back to the TV which was running a trailer for *Parkinson*. "What's on next?"

"No idea," said Jimmy. "Neither of us could be bothered to go out and get a paper, remember?"

"Pretty poor show from two journalists," said Keith, as he watched the spinning blue and yellow globe on the screen that came on at the start of every BBC programme. He had enjoyed seeing this again as well as all the logos of the different TV companies. From the wavy lines of London Weekend Television to the proud silver knight of Anglia before *Sale of the Century*, they seemed like an integral part of the shows they introduced. What a pity they had done away with all the regional ITV stations.

"It's *Dallas*!" he exclaimed, as the BBC globe faded away to be replaced by a scene of classic 1970s cars speeding along a freeway towards the gleaming silver skyscrapers of the American dream.

"I'm not into *Dallas*, said Jimmy. "I've only seen it a couple of times. We're normally out on the piss when it's on."

"You must be joking!" said Keith. "*Dallas* is huge! Have they figured out who shot JR yet?"

"Which one's JR?" asked Jimmy, as the opening credits reached the point where the cast began appearing. "Is he the one with the hat?"

"They've all got hats!" said Keith, annoyed at Jimmy's inane comments.

"She hasn't," replied Jimmy, looking at the three pictures of Linda Gray on the screen, in the split-screen format that was unique to the show.

"Don't be obtuse, Jimmy. Look, that's him!" he added as Larry Hagman appeared, grinning away, no doubt at the expense of some business rival he had just scuppered.

"Can't say he rings any bells. And someone shot him, you say?"

"Yes. Or rather they will. Perhaps that hasn't happened yet." *It can't have*, he thought, *or else Jimmy would have heard about it.*

"How do you know about it, then?"

"Oh, if only you knew, Jimmy if only you knew," he replied. The mystery of who shot JR was going to be huge, and what's more, he was sure it was happening soon. If only he had a head for dates. All he could remember was it had been all over the papers and he had worked on the story. It was one of the biggest events in the history of television, and he knew it was going to happen before anyone else. How could he make use of that information?

"Perhaps we should watch *Dallas* more often," he said. "I have a feeling it could come in handy later this year."

"I'm not staying in every Saturday just to watch some American soap opera," said Jimmy.

"Maybe we could get hold of some tapes from the guys who do the TV listings at the paper," said Keith "They get advance review copies of all sorts of stuff. Then we could watch them when we want."

"We've got nothing to play them on," said Jimmy.

"We'll get a video machine."

"You must be joking. Do you know how much those things cost? Five hundred quid! How do you suggest paying for that on ninety quid each a week?"

"I didn't realise they were that much," said Keith, marvelling at how expensive new tech could be. Twenty years from now, it would be possible to pick up a cheap one from Argos for about thirty pounds but at this time they were the preserve of the wealthy.

Ninety quid a week was indeed not a lot to live on and Keith's joy at discovering beer was less than 50p a pint was soon tempered when he realised how little he got paid each week.

"We could hire one, I suppose," said Jimmy. "Radio Rentals do them for twenty quid a month. But I don't see the point. We're out most nights. We wouldn't get our money's worth. Anyway, look, you've distracted me, going on about *Dallas*. Let's get back to the subject of my medicinal hard liquor. What have we got in?"

"Not a lot," replied Keith. "Other than beer, we're pretty much out of booze. Unless you fancy that revolting advocaat stuff that's been sitting on the windowsill for weeks. I don't know what possessed you to buy that."

"I didn't. It's the only thing left over from the flat-warming party we had in November. Tight Terry brought it, do you remember?"

"Ah, yeah, that's right," said Keith, who did remember the party despite it being over forty years ago for him. "He tried to make out he'd bought it himself but I reckon someone gave it to his gran the previous Christmas, then he swiped it when she carked it."

"I wouldn't put it past him. There's nothing else for it, then. You'll have to go to the off-licence."

"Bloody hell, why me?"

"Because I'm ill, remember?" said Jimmy, adding a couple of coughs for dramatic effect. "Get some whisky. No, scratch that, let's go for brandy. That's what they always give invalids, isn't it? A drop of brandy, that's the thing."

"Very well. Anything else?"

"Yeah, twenty Silk Cut. And some pork scratchings. Got to keep my strength up."

"Fuck's sake, Jimmy, you'll be lucky to see fifty the way you're going," said Keith, though he knew this wasn't true. Jimmy was still alive and had made it into his sixties in the future. Much to Keith's annoyance, apart from being overweight he was seemingly the picture of health in 2019 despite never cutting back on his unhealthy lifestyle. He didn't seem to have the same problems as Keith with his bladder either.

The local Oddbins wasn't far, just at the end of their road. When Keith got back, Jimmy was engrossed in *Dallas*.

"Blimey, this JR's a right bastard, isn't he?" said Jimmy, unable to tear his eyes away from the screen.

"I told you. He's going to get shot. It's going to be the murder mystery of all time because, by the time it happens, he's crapped on practically everyone in the show."

"I reckon it'll be his wife. He treats her like shit."

"Umm, I'm not sure," said Keith, struggling to remember. He had known at the time but it was all so long ago. Well that was bloody useless, wasn't it? He could have broken the story in the paper before anyone else. That would have given his career a real boost.

66

He hadn't made much use of his future knowledge to make his mark at the paper during his first month. The problem was that he just wasn't a stickler for dates unless it was something huge, and 1980 wasn't a year that stuck in his mind. If only it had been 1981. That was the year that Prince Charles was going to get engaged and marry Lady Diana Spencer. Now that would have been a scoop if he could have revealed it before anyone else! But he was a year early.

Most of the news stories that had arisen during January 1980 he barely remembered, and even if something did jog his memory, it was too late by the time the story came in. There was a lot of stuff about the recent Russian invasion of Afghanistan, hostages in Tehran, plus a steel workers' strike, but nothing he could get his teeth into. So, he just kept abreast of things hoping that something bigger would come along and give him an opportunity at some point.

Then, that night, after he and Jimmy had polished off half a bottle of Napoleon brandy between them, things finally started to happen.

Keith didn't dream much and if he did he rarely remembered the content. But that night, he had a dream so vivid that when he woke up he recalled it as well as if he had just been sitting in a cinema for two hours engrossed in a film.

It had started bizarrely with him watching ice skating. Now why would he be dreaming about that? Keith despised ice skating, especially that *Dancing on Ice* rubbish on the television. A few years ago he had been forced to watch a few hours of it ahead of interviewing the winner on his radio show. As for it being classed as a sport, that was debatable in his opinion. When the Winter Olympics came on, he liked to watch the downhill skiing. That was fast and furious and came with the occasional bonus of a spectacular crash. It was proper competition, and worth watching. But figure skating, which was all about the opinion of some judges? No thanks.

He wasn't sure who he was watching at first or what competition it was. In the dream, he tried to remember who Britain's famous skaters of the past had been. There was Torvill and Dean of course. Everyone knew Torvill and Dean but it obviously wasn't them as this was just a bloke on his own. Who else was there? Some bloke called Curry. Was it Tim? No, that wasn't right. Tim Curry was an actor. Maybe it was John. Bloody hell, his memory was useless.

He was put out of his misery when the name of the skater flashed up on the screen, next to a crude representation of the Union flag, which was the best the primitive graphics of the time could muster. This was accompanied by some very positive-looking scores from the judges. Of course, this was Robin Cousins and this was him winning the gold medal at the Winter Olympics.

Then, bizarrely, the dream shifted to a suburban street in London, where the very same Robin Cousins was coming out of a café, and heading towards a zebra crossing. Just as he began to cross, a red Ford Capri screeched around the corner, hotly pursued by a police car. The nimble-footed skater turned to try to get out of the way, and almost succeeded, but in the end the Capri ran over his right foot.

Next, the dream cut to a scene of Cousins having a broken toe bandaged up in casualty, followed by a final scene back at the Olympics again where Robin was nowhere to be seen, and some East German guy was being awarded the medal instead. Then Keith woke up.

The first thing he noticed was that the bracelet was lit up and pulsing, a light red. Reflecting on the dream, it wasn't difficult to figure out what all this was about. He had been shown two possible futures. The correct timeline, in which Robin Cousins had won the gold medal at the Winter Olympics. And an alternate reality, when through no fault of his own he had become incapacitated leaving him unable to participate.

Was this what he had been sent here to do? Did he need to ensure Britain's top skater made it to the Olympics to claim the gold medal that was rightfully his? With all due respect to Robin, it was hardly world-changing stuff.

Jimmy was already up and watching the Open University when Keith stumbled through to the living area in search of coffee, so he decided to pick his brains, assuming that there was anything in there to pick.

"Morning, Jimmy. Listen, mate, when's the Winter Olympics?"

"In a couple of weeks, I think. The BBC have been running trailers for it."

"Do you know anything about this Robin Cousins guy?"

"Is he the bloke who does *Question Time*?"

"That's Robin Day, you idiot."

"Sorry, I don't then," replied Jimmy, before descending into a coughing fit that reverberated around the flat so loudly Keith feared it might cause actual structural damage.

"The brandy and Silk Cut cure worked well, then," he observed drily.

"Perhaps the smokes weren't strong enough. I should have had one of your Marlboros. Or maybe a cigar."

"Are you going to be fit enough for work tonight? We're due in at six to help put Monday's edition together, remember?"

"I don't think so. I feel dreadful. Can you go out and get me some Night Nurse?"

"From where? Everything's bloody shut on Sundays, remember?"

Keith had grown to loathe Sundays over the past month. There was nothing to do for most of the day. Nothing on the telly in the morning other than the Open University or religious programmes. No shops open. No football, rugby, or horse racing. Betting on the Sabbath was against the law. It was a sporting and cultural desert. If it were not for the pubs it would have scarcely been worth getting up but even they were only open for two hours from twelve until two. Then it was an interminable five-hour wait until they reopened at seven.

The only thing worth doing in that dull stretch of time was listening to the Top 40 at teatime on Radio One, presented by Tony Blackburn. Keith had been lucky enough to arrive in a truly golden era for pop music, and since he had been here he had enjoyed hearing Pink

70

Floyd, The Pretenders and The Specials occupying the number one spot. What a time to be alive! But equally, what the hell had gone wrong since? No one in the modern day could hold a candle to these artists.

He left Jimmy feeling sorry for himself on the pretext of trying to find a pharmacy that was open on a Sunday but in truth, he was just slipping off to the pub for a pint and a game of *Space Invaders*. Annoyingly, the bracelet had gone quiet on him. If it wanted him to help Robin, it might help if it told him when and where to go. How was he to know where some random road crossing was and when to be there? It could be anywhere in London. Or even further afield.

The pub he frequented at the opposite end of the street to the off-licence was a real old-fashioned haunt called The Canterbury. It was on a corner and had been lovingly tiled in red all over by a craftsman who clearly took pride in his work. Its regular visitors were largely locals, with tourists tending to shun this none-too-salubrious end of Whitechapel. It had a real sense of community, another thing that he felt had declined over the years. He dreaded to think what had happened to this establishment in the long term but he was willing to bet it was no longer a pub. More than likely, it was now just another identikit outlet of one of the ubiquitous coffee shop or fast-food chains.

Jimmy did not recover in time to make it into work and there were no more clues from the bracelet. When Keith arrived at work, he made use of the newsroom's extensive resources to find out as much about Robin Cousins and the upcoming Olympics as he could. Then

71

he made a beeline for Jerry, to see if he could get assigned to cover the event.

"Evening, Jerry, how's it going?"

"What do you want, Diamond? I'm busy." To emphasise his point, he didn't look up from his desk where he was proofreading an article line by line using an old wooden ruler.

"I was just wondering if we were going to be covering the Winter Olympics in the paper?"

Jerry looked up from his work, a knowing look on his face. "You can stop right there, lad. I know your game. You're after a free trip to New York, aren't you? Well, you're not on. If we do report on any of the events, the television coverage will be quite sufficient."

"What do you mean, if?"

"It's only the Winter Olympics? I mean, we don't exactly set the world alight at it, do we? How many British champion downhill skiers do you know? Hardly get a chance for much practice on the two days a year it snows in England, do they?"

"What about this chap Robin Cousins?"

"Who's he?"

"Come on, Jerry, you must know who Robin Cousins is. He's just won the European figure skating championships and is in with a good shot at winning gold at Lake Placid."

Keith had found out this information by looking through the previous week's copies of the more cerebral broadsheet dailies. As a matter of course they took all the rival papers every day, then archived them using a microfiche system that would allow them to reference old stories whenever they needed to.

"Look, Keith, our readers are not interested in ice skating. Racing and football, that's all they care about. And the odd bit of boxing. Do you think the average builder who likes looking at the tits and football results on his tea break in the morning is interested in some bloke in tights dancing to classical music? We leave reporting on all that poncey stuff to *The Times* and *The Guardian*."

"What about John Curry? He won last time. You must have put something in the paper about that."

"Ah, yeah, I suppose so. After he'd won, not before. Plucky Brit comes good, that sort of thing. Got to be patriotic, haven't you?"

"Exactly, and that's why I want to interview Robin Cousins because he's going to win too. It'll be a real scoop for us."

"How do you know he's going to win?"

"I just do, that's all."

"Sorry, that's not good enough. Now since you've obviously got nothing better to do you can do the race cards for tomorrow's meetings at Plumpton and Kempton."

"Bloody hell," said Keith, who hated doing the racing. That meant doing the tips too, which he knew bugger all about so he normally just looked at the betting forecast they got sent to them from *The Sporting Life* and picked all the favourites. Usually at least a couple would come in.

By the time he got home Jimmy was in bed, and Keith was still none the wiser as to how he was supposed to protect Robin from the car chase. During the night, he had the same dream as the previous night, but how was that supposed to help him? He awoke to see the bracelet pulsing red again, which was some sort of warning, but it might as well have been a twinkling fairy light on a Christmas tree for all the good it was doing him. He needed some concrete help.

Jimmy seemed a little better. Over a breakfast of Ricicles, which was all they had left in the house, topped with milk that was on the brink of the turn, he declared that he would be back at work in the afternoon. It was shortly after passing himself fit for duty that the bracelet began pulsing again, and this time it was different.

The jewel was flashing a much brighter red colour than before at regular intervals, a second apart. The implication was clear. If it had emitted sound as well, it would be as if an alarm had gone off. It was red alert time, and once again Keith could feel the device reaching into his mind. He could picture himself leaving the flat with Jimmy and walking up the road towards the nearest Tube station with the bracelet directing him where to go. As it continued to flash, a thought occurred to him. There could be an opportunity here, both for him and Jimmy.

"Grab your camera, Jimmy. We've got work to do."

"What do you mean? We don't start until after lunch on Mondays."

"Today we do. I've got a hunch that if we're in the right place and right time later, you'll get that killer shot you're always talking about."

74

"What sort of hunch? I don't want to go out yet. I'll miss *Rainbow*."

"Trust me, Jimmy, you get this right and you'll be top dog in the newsroom tonight. Now, come on."

Accompanied by a reluctant and grumbling companion, Keith left the flat a few minutes later as the bracelet continued to flash the urgent red warning. Wherever they were going, it seemed time was of the essence. Why couldn't the blasted thing have given him a bit more notice? Weeks of inactivity and now it was all last-minute panic.

"Where are we going?" asked Jimmy, as they hurried up the road towards Whitechapel Station, all the time getting drizzled on by the leaden grey skies that had hung over London for weeks.

"You'll see," said Keith, who hadn't a clue himself, but was allowing the bracelet to guide him. Not only was it giving him a sense of which way to go, but it was acknowledging his choices with brief green flashes each time he made the correct decision. Before long, they found themselves on the westbound platform of the Hammersmith and City line.

Once on the train, the bracelet seemed to calm down a bit as they trundled westward through the heart of the city. It was still glowing red, but not flashing as it had been before. Several times Jimmy pestered him as to where they were going, and it was hard for Keith to keep fending him off with enigmatic answers. Eventually, as they approached White City, the bracelet switched to flashing green at him. It was telling him it was time to get off.

"This is our stop," he said, as the train slowed to a halt.

"About bloody time," replied Jimmy. "This had better be worth it."

"Oh, it will be," said Keith, hoping fervently that it would. Finally, it seemed he was going to find out if the bracelet was all it had been cracked up to be.

Keith knew the area well, as he and Jimmy had often come to spend the evening at the White City dog track in the past, but he still couldn't identify the exact location of the street in his dream. This didn't matter, though, because the bracelet continued to guide him, and just a couple of minutes after leaving the station they turned into the street where he expected all the action to unfold.

"This is it, Jimmy," he said, stopping close to the edge of the zebra crossing he had seen in his dream. "You set yourself up right here and train your camera on that corner. That's where it's all going to kick off. Meanwhile, I'm just popping over to that café."

He had spotted the place he was expecting Robin to emerge from. Judging by the way the bracelet was now flashing green, he was on the right track.

"What? You go for a coffee while I stay out here in the rain?"

"Just do it, Jimmy," insisted Keith, making his way to the door. Just before he got there, it opened, and the living legend that was Robin Cousins emerged. As he did, Keith immediately accosted him.

"Mr Cousins? My name's Keith Diamond, I'm a reporter from one of the dailies. May I congratulate you on your recent success in the European Championships?

I was wondering if you might have a word or two for our readers ahead of your upcoming Olympic bid."

Robin proved to be a most affable young man and as Keith kept him talking, he heard the roar of the approaching Capri. He looked over his shoulder to see it speeding towards the crossing, almost hitting Jimmy in the process as he snapped away at the car chase taking place right in front of him.

"My goodness, look at that!" remarked Keith, as the Capri swerved and crashed into a row of parked cars about fifty yards past the crossing. This part was new to him as his dream had not extended that far.

"Lucky we were over here out of the way, eh, Mr Cousins? We could have got hurt! Anyway, lovely chatting to you, I must go and see if my friend is OK."

And with that, he left a somewhat bemused Robin to go safely on his way, re-joining Jimmy who was now busy photographing the police who were dragging the dazed robbers from the wrecked car and apprehending them.

"Wow!" said Jimmy. "But how did you know?"

"Anonymous tip-off," said Keith, hoping this would suffice. He looked down at the bracelet which was now glowing a solid bright green with approval. And so it should. He had made a decent fist of this, all things considered.

Jimmy was happy enough with the pictures he had taken to accept Keith's explanation, and when they got back to the newsroom their day got better as they excitedly told the tale of how they had witnessed and photographed the incident. It was already known about in the newsroom where a report had come in from one of the news agencies about a bank robbery in Shepherd's Bush. With the photos and Keith's eyewitness report, they made the front page of Tuesday's edition.

What was it Elizabeth had warned him about when she had first passed on the bracelet to him? Not to do anything for personal gain? Well, it certainly didn't seem to be concerned that he and Jimmy had taken advantage of the situation to further their careers. Perhaps that was because it had all been in the line of duty, a fringe benefit, one could say. If doing a good deed meant a scoop on a major story which contributed to better career prospects in the long term, it seemed that this was well within the rules.

A couple of weeks later, Keith put aside his dislike of figure skating and tuned in to watch Robin's tremendous performance to bring home the gold medal.

It still didn't seem a big deal in the grand scheme of things. Surely he couldn't have been sent back in time just for this? Why was this one event so important? Perhaps Robin's victory would inspire some undiscovered skating talent to do great things in the future. But to be honest, he couldn't remember there being any more famous skaters after the 1980s. Perhaps it was something less obvious, such as encouraging local councils to invest more in sporting facilities for the benefit of all. But he didn't know. Perhaps he never would.

Whatever the reason, it gave him a great deal of satisfaction, even if the rest of the world would never know of his contribution. He had done something to make a difference and proved his capability in performing the tasks he had been sent here to do.

What came next, he had no idea, but he had the distinct feeling that much bigger things were on the way.

March 1980

"He wants you to do what?" asked Jimmy incredulously.

"He wants me to go around and interview a doctor who wants to spill the beans about things he's removed from famous people's bottoms."

"And he wants me to go too?"

"Yes, to take pictures. Thinks it might be worth a double spread tomorrow."

"Pictures of what, precisely? I mean, this is a family newspaper, Keith. Don't you think this is a tad puerile, even by our standards?"

"You know what Jerry's like. If it boosts circulation, he'll print any old crap."

"I'm not sure I appreciate your choice of word, given the subject matter," replied Jimmy. "Honestly, is this the sort of thing you envisaged us doing when we came to work here?"

"Come on, Jimmy, you can't be that naïve. We knew what we were getting into when we applied for the red tops. At your insistence, if I recall correctly. I thought we'd be better off writing for the music press, but you were adamant. You said, 'tits, not hits,' if I recall correctly."

"Yes, and we've been here six months and I haven't had so much as a sniff of Page 3 yet," said Jimmy. "And now here we are writing stories about celebrity arses."

"Well, they did say we'd be starting at the bottom, didn't they?" quipped a smiling Keith.

"Dreadful," replied Jimmy. "Have you ever considered a career in stand-up comedy? Because my advice is, don't."

"Yes, well forgive me if I don't take advice from the most humourless man in London. Now, I suggest we get going."

They were sitting together at Keith's desk in the unusually quiet newsroom. It was mid-afternoon and most of the journalists were normally back from the pub by now. Perhaps they had moved on to an afternoon drinking club. It wasn't unheard of. He knew that Bob and Gordon were members of an underground club called The Colchester, just around the corner. Perhaps they had gone there.

Keith could scarcely believe he had been in 1980 for nearly three months. Time had flown by, and apart from the Robin Cousins episode, he had still done hardly anything noteworthy when it came to keeping history on track.

He had managed to do plenty of other things, though. The highlight was a trip to see his beloved Clash play at the Lewisham Odeon in February. It had whetted his appetite to see as many bands as he could, and since the Clash gig he had also seen Joy Division, Killing Joke, and Squeeze.

Revisiting past haunts had been a lot of fun, but something else had been playing on his mind. Being back here in 1980 had made him think about his family history. Up until the mid-seventies his childhood and teenage years had been happy ones but that all changed when his mother died of breast cancer during the scorching summer of 1976. He had just finished his A-levels and what should have been one of the best years of his life turned into one of searing pain and misery. But there had been further heartbreak to come.

His connection with his father had always been distant, and far from being united in grief, they drifted further apart. After he left for university in Sheffield in September 1976, contact between them was sporadic. When he returned to Watford in December, he found his father living with a hard-faced woman from Dundee. After an uncomfortable Christmas, during which he had felt distinctly unwelcome, he returned to his campus and by Easter he was effectively homeless. The house had been sold, his father had moved to Scotland, and it was clear that his presence was no longer required.

He stayed in his student halls over Easter because he had nowhere else to go. In the summer Jimmy, whom he had met at university, suggested they share a flat. This was an arrangement that continued after they had moved down to London until another life-changing event led to a further upheaval. That change was yet to happen but he knew the seeds of it would be sown before the end of this year and he would have to confront it when the time came. But for now, his more immediate thoughts lay with his family.

Should he reach out to his father and try to build bridges? Would he even care, or was he too busy cosying up to his Scottish girlfriend? He looked to the bracelet for guidance but it had none to offer. It was very difficult navigating this strange journey through the past whilst trying to stick to the ambiguous rules he had been given. Change things, but don't change things. Improve your life, but don't take advantage. It was all way too cryptic but it seemed in this case he was being given a free choice.

Ultimately, he decided to leave well alone. What was the point? And there was no one else in the family to turn to. His grandparents were already gone, and he was an only child. There were a few aunts and uncles dotted about, but no one he had any real desire to see. He had pretty much been on his own since his mother's death and couldn't see how being back here in 1980 was going to change that. Even when he had been married he had felt alone. And none of his many casual encounters helped much. They were short-term fixes for a seemingly unresolvable problem.

All he really had was Jimmy. Good old annoying, idiotic Jimmy who infuriated him every day, yet somehow was the closest thing he had to family. It was an arrangement that was destined to endure throughout the decades. Despite life taking them in different directions at times, they always ended up back together in some capacity. Whether it was working, living, or just socialising, their lives were intrinsically entwined, almost like an old married couple. Much as he maligned and teased his flatmate, he was fonder of him than he would ever admit.

The assignment they had been sent on didn't ring any bells from Keith's previous stint in 1980. This reinforced his earlier assumption that his mere presence in the past was already reshaping his life, and sending him in different directions. Their task today was to interview a certain Doctor Harold Monkfish, residing at a Walthamstow address, near the dog track. It didn't sound glamorous, and it certainly wasn't.

On arrival, Jimmy squinted at the dilapidated semidetached house before them. "Are you sure this is the right address? It doesn't look like the sort of place where a doctor would live."

Keith surveyed the scene, agreeing wholeheartedly. The front garden was a sorry mix of cracked paving stones, bare lawn, and an array of unruly weeds, from dandelions to a thistle nearly as tall as he was. Here and there, patches of the original lawn were struggling to survive but appeared to be losing the battle. Empty glass bottles, many broken, littered the ground, including an intact bottle of dandelion and burdock, which had appropriately come to rest in a patch of dandelions.

The exterior condition of the house mirrored the garden. Most striking were the peeling wooden window frames and windows that looked as though they hadn't been cleaned since the Blitz. To complete the picture of decay, a rusting old fridge had been abandoned next to the side gate, with a couple of old tyres propped against it for good measure.

As they hesitated, contemplating what to do, the front door creaked open in the style of something from a Hammer Horror movie and the decision was made for them.

"Mr Diamond?" inquired the man who opened the door, a slight, dark-haired fellow aged about forty, with wiry glasses and wearing the standard-issue white lab coat sported by television doctors.

"Well, he looks like a doctor," said Jimmy, opening the gate which made a horrible grating noise even worse than the front door. Keith wasn't convinced. There was something about the man that seemed familiar but as was frequently the case, the details eluded him after so many years. He wasn't going to find out standing outside on the pavement, so with a hint of trepidation, he followed Jimmy inside.

He was right to be wary; the house was cluttered to the point of claustrophobia. The floor, from what they could see of it, was carpeted but covered with fluff and crumbs suggesting it hadn't been vacuumed for some time, if ever. The reason for the lack of floor space was the presence of countless piles of magazines scattered everywhere. It appeared that Harold had been collecting every periodical ever produced, judging by the sheer number. These stacks contained issues of numerous publications, from *Time* magazine to the *New Scientist*.

"Wow, this is quite a collection you have here," remarked Jimmy, as Harold led them into his living room.

"Yes, well one must keep up with the latest developments in the world of science and nature," he replied. "Please take a seat."

"If we can find one," said Keith. With some difficulty, they managed to squeeze themselves onto the sofa, in between piles of *National Geographic* magazines.

"Cup of tea?" asked Harold.

"Oh, yes, please," said Jimmy.

"I'll pass if you don't mind," said Keith, casting his eye around the room and deciding against it.

"Very well," said Harold, disappearing off into the kitchen, giving them a moment to talk.

"Are you insane?" said Keith, speaking in a low voice just above a whisper so he wouldn't be overheard. "Because he clearly is. You never accept a cup of tea in a place like this."

"Oh, come on, he's harmless. What do you think he's going to do, poison me?"

"Perhaps. Look at the state of this room. What do you imagine the kitchen's going to be like? It's hardly going to get a 5-star food hygiene rating is it?"

He knew this reference would go over Jimmy's head, as such ratings didn't exist at this time, but he still got the gist.

"Oh come on, it's no worse than ours."

"Oh it is, and that's saying something. What the hell are we doing here? This bloke's a nutter."

"Well, since we are here we may as well see what he's got to say."

"Milk and sugar?" called Harold from the kitchen.

"Three please," said Jimmy.

"Greedy bastard," said Keith. "Better hope it's just sugar and not rat poison. Remember that story a few weeks ago? The Peckham Poisoner?"

"Oh, yeah," said Jimmy, suddenly looking nervous as Harold came back in with the tea, which was served in a chipped pale green mug that looked like standard hospital issue. It didn't do anything to convince Keith that he might be a doctor. Perhaps he had smuggled the mug out of the nearest asylum.

After a brief bit of chit-chat about the weather, Keith attempted to steer the conversation toward the intended topic, allowing Harold to open up.

"Oh, yes, you wouldn't believe the things I've seen. Have a look at this," he said, opening a drawer in a sideboard and pulling out a muscular rubbery action figure with tanned plastic skin and a smiling face.

"Do you know what this is?" he asked.

Keith hadn't a clue, but Jimmy chimed in.

"I do," he said. "It's a Stretch Armstrong. I bought one for my nephew last Christmas."

"Quite right," said Harold, pulling at one of the legs and stretching out the malleable gel-like material. "And do you want to know where I found it?"

"Go on," said Keith, his voice heavy with scepticism, watching as Stretch Armstrong's leg slowly regained its shape.

"Well, you know that actor from the Carry On films?"

"Which one?"

"This one," said Harold, reaching into the same drawer, pulling out a poster featuring the cast, and pointing at one of the stars.

"Oh, him," said Jimmy. "That doesn't surprise me."

"Yes, so, he presented at casualty one night, complaining of bowel pain, and when I investigated, I retrieved this. Do you want to take a picture of it?"

"No, we don't," said Keith. "I'm afraid I don't believe a word of it."

"OK, well how about this then," said Harold, reaching into the drawer and producing a craggy, misshapen lump of rock roughly resembling a phallus.

"What's that?" asked Keith wearily.

"It's moon rock," said Harold. "Very rare."

"Moon rock?" asked Jimmy. "How did you get hold of it?"

"Well, I am sure you remember when the astronauts went to the moon. Let's face it, there's not a lot to do up there, is there? So when they wandered out onto the surface, they were looking for something to alleviate the boredom. So, to cut a long story short, when they got back, I was one of the medical team at NASA assigned to check them over. And when…"

"OK, we've heard enough," said Keith, who could see where this was going a mile off. "Come on, Jimmy, we're leaving."

"Oh, don't go," said Harold. "I haven't had a chance to tell you about this yet," he said, producing a large cactus plant, much to Keith's chagrin.

"Where did that come from, *Little House on the Prairie*? I've never heard such juvenile nonsense in all my life."

"But you haven't drunk your tea yet!" protested Harold.

"Um, I think I'll pass if you don't mind," said Jimmy, thoughts of the Peckham Poisoner on his mind.

They couldn't get out of the house quickly enough and it was only when they turned the corner out of the street that they recovered enough to speak.

"That was utterly ridiculous," said Keith. "What on earth was Jerry thinking?"

"You know, in hindsight, I'm not sure if he was a real doctor after all," remarked Jimmy.

"Of course he wasn't a real doctor," replied Keith, putting his head in his hands in frustration at Jimmy's gullibility. "That white coat was all part of his delusion. And why would he wear it at home anyway? Come on, we had better get back and give them the bad news that we've got nothing for tomorrow's paper."

Getting back proved more difficult than anticipated. When they got to the Tube station it was to discover that all trains on the Victoria Line had been suspended due to an incident at Finsbury Park.

"We're going to have to phone the office and let them know what's happened," said Keith, wandering into a shopping street hoping to find a phone box. "What time is it?"

"Just gone six," said Jimmy, glancing at his watch. "It'll be dark soon."

"Come on, then," said Keith, spotting a traditional red telephone box ahead. As much as he enjoyed these simpler times, there were disadvantages to not being permanently connected to the world. He couldn't deny it was nice not being at the beck and call of everyone constantly, particularly once they left the office. Once they were out and about, no one could keep tabs on them. Unfortunately, this worked both ways and when they needed to get hold of someone in a hurry, the antiquated nature of the communications network made Keith wonder how anything ever got done.

Nothing was going to get done in this box. The handset was missing. It looked as if someone had ripped it off the side of the phone, complete with cable, and then stolen it. For what purpose, Keith had no idea. As for the inside of the box, it had been decorated with the calling cards of every prostitute in London. Well, they weren't going to be getting any business from this box.

"We'll have to find another one," suggested Jimmy.

"Genius," replied Keith sarcastically. "What would I do without you?"

The next box, a hundred yards or so up the street, was also no use to them. It contained a small puddle which from the smell of it could only be urine. As for the phone, although it appeared to be intact, it was completely dead. There was no dialling tone at all. It too was peppered with cards offering dubious services such as French polishing.

The third box, other than a couple of smashed windows, appeared to be in order. It was only when Keith went to put a twopence piece in the slot that he realised the problem. Some wanker had stuffed chewing gum into the coin slot rendering it unusable. Why did people do these things?

Finally, as darkness began to fall, they found a working phone. Unfortunately, there was a man inside talking, and a woman waiting to use it after him. Given that it was the only functioning box in the area, and with it being past 6pm which was when the cheaper rate began, it was inevitable that it would be in high demand.

The bloke in the box was in there for about five minutes, though it seemed like longer. When he finally came out, the middle-aged lady who had been there before them went in. Any hope that she wouldn't be long gradually faded as several minutes passed. Why did people spend so much time in phone boxes, especially when they knew other people were waiting? It was bloody rude, in Keith's opinion.

He paced around, attempting to catch her attention through the glass, but she turned away. Undeterred, he started circling the box, determined to make his presence felt, and then he noticed something peculiar.

"Look at this, Jimmy," he said, waving his friend over, who had taken a seat in a nearby bus shelter out of sheer boredom.

"What is it?"

"Look at that woman in there. She's not saying anything. She's just holding the phone to her ear and not speaking."

"So?"

"So either the other person is rabbiting nineteen to the dozen or there is no one on the other end at all."

"Ask her, then."

"I will," said Keith determinedly, rapping firmly on the glass door pane. "Excuse me, are you going to be much longer?"

The door opened and the woman spoke, in a distinctly unfriendly tone.

"Do you mind? I'm waiting for my sister."

"What do you mean, you're waiting for your sister? This is a phone box."

"Yes, and I am waiting to speak to her."

91

"Sorry, that doesn't make any sense. You've been in there ten minutes. If she hasn't answered by now, then I doubt she's going to."

"You don't understand. I'm waiting for her."

"Yes, you said that already, love. What exactly do you mean?"

"Look, it's perfectly simple. My sister lives in Guildford, but she's not on the phone."

"How are you ringing her, then?"

"Her friend is on the phone. I ring her, and then she goes to get my sister from her house."

"And how long does that take?"

"Not long. She's only in the next street."

"The next street?"

"Well, next but one."

"But that must cost you a fortune. You could have paid for a bus to visit her by now."

"Oh, I don't mind. It's family, isn't it? Ooh, wait, I think she's here? Gladys? Is that you? What? Oh, no, just some impatient young man who wants to use the phone box. What? Yes, he will have to wait, won't he? I don't know, the youth of today."

With that, she shut the door in his face.

"You know what, Jimmy. I've had enough of this. Today has turned into a dead loss."

"Why don't we try that pub over there? They might have a phone."

"That, my friend, is the most sensible thing you have said all day."

It was a pub neither of them had frequented before. To Keith's annoyance, when asking about the phone they were informed by the barman that use of it was reserved for regulars only. They circumnavigated that rule by sweetening him up with the offer of a couple of drinks which meant that at last Keith got through to the newsroom. When he did, he received a stern interrogation.

"Where the bloody hell are you, Diamond? You should have been back here ages ago."

"Yes, I'm sorry about that, Jerry. The Tube's not running."

"Wait, what's that noise?" asked Jerry, detecting the background hubbub around Keith. "Are you in a pub? When you're supposed to be working?"

It was hardly the crime of the century, thought Keith. Half of Fleet Street spent half their lives in the pub. Perhaps he had better try to explain.

"All the phone boxes have been vandalised. We only came in here to call you, but listen. You know that guy you sent us to see? He was a complete nutter. He wasn't even a doctor. That story was all bollocks."

"Hahahaha!" guffawed Jerry down the phone. "Here, listen to this, lads," he added, clearly addressing everyone back in the office. "Keith and Jimmy have just become the latest victims of Mad Harry!"

And then Keith heard a lot of laughing and cheering coming down the line from the others in the newsroom, who were clearly enjoying a great deal of amusement at their expense.

"What?" said Keith. Who was Mad Harry? And then he finally remembered. He had seen the man before.

"Bloody hell, Jerry."

"Got you good and proper, there, didn't I? Listen, lads, I don't need you in here tonight. Relax and have a drink and we'll see you both tomorrow."

And then he rang off, still laughing.

"What was that all about?" said Jimmy, unable to hear Jerry's side of the conversation.

"We've been the victims of a wind-up," said Keith, finally remembering who Mad Harry was. For whatever reason, he and Jimmy had escaped this humiliation in the original timeline, supporting his hypothesis that the ripples he had created were making day-to-day events play out differently. However, years later, by which time Keith knew of Harry's reputation, he had helped orchestrate a similar prank on someone else.

"A wind-up by whom? Doctor Harold?"

"Well, indirectly, but facilitated by Jerry. Doctor Harold, as you call him, is more commonly known as Mad Harry. He contacts the paper about once a year with some insane story trying to get it published. He's been doing it for years. It's become such a tradition that instead of fobbing him off, the editors send a couple of the unsuspecting new boys around to humour him."

"And that's us?"

"Yes, that's us. I can't believe we fell for it."

"Why didn't you mention it earlier?"

"I forgot until now. It was only when Jerry told me, I remembered that Ted told me about Mad Harry when

94

we first started. Still, look on the bright side. He's given us the evening off now. We may as well stay here for an hour or two until they get the trains up and running again."

"Sounds good to me," said Jimmy. "Look, there's one of those table games over there. Fancy it?"

"Come on then," said Keith. He had been enjoying playing the old video games, and the table versions they had put in pubs were a genius idea. You could sit opposite a friend, have a couple of pints of Skol, and play a game at the same time. Whatever had happened to these? They had seemed like a great invention because they didn't take up any extra room like a cabinet game would. Nonetheless, they had completely disappeared after the 1980s.

The game was *Galaxian*, and Keith preferred that to *Space Invaders*. It had more variation in the gameplay and over a lengthy session, he beat Jimmy by seven games to three. After they left the pub they made their way home, stopping off at The Canterbury when they got back to Whitechapel, leading to the inevitable hangover the next day. This meant they were not in the best shape when they made it to work where they were subject to a barrage of piss-taking over the previous day's incident. As he took his place next to Ted, the veteran journalist took Keith to task.

"I warned you about Mad Harry when you first started," said Ted. "I can't believe you fell for it."

"Sorry, Ted," said Keith, grateful for his mentor's warning, even if he hadn't heeded it. "I just forgot. But thanks for trying. I owe you one."

"I'll hold you to that, lad," said Ted, before descending into a coughing fit. Unlike Jimmy's similar symptoms when he was spreading his germs all over the flat, Keith knew this wasn't a temporary bout that could be attributed to a bad cold. Ted did this all the time. As he spluttered away, Keith noticed the bracelet glowing red. It was the first time it had done anything for days. Where had it been yesterday when he was trying to find a phone box? It hadn't fancied directing him to one then, had it?

Keith genuinely liked Ted. He was one of the few decent sorts in a room full of arseholes. If he was being brutally honest, he and Jimmy were probably two of them. If anyone deserved a happy retirement it was Ted, but Keith knew that his future wasn't looking rosy. Perhaps it was time he tried to do something about it, and the bracelet agreed, changing from red to green as it followed his train of thought.

"Listen, Ted, you really ought to get that cough looked at."

"There's nothing wrong with me that a drop of this won't cure," replied Ted, reaching into his desk, pulling out his trusty bottle of Scotch, and blatantly taking a swig, without being in the slightest bit bothered if anyone saw him. Most of the alcoholics in the newsroom at least made some token effort to hide their habit but Ted didn't care anymore.

"When do you retire, Ted?"

"Why, are you after my job? You'll have to wait another year. I turn sixty-five next summer. Then I'm out of here with a big fat pension and big plans."

"Like what?"

"I'm getting out of this country for a start. I reckon it's finished. I mean look at it, industry failing, rampant inflation, soaring unemployment. They said it would get better once Maggie got in but if you ask me, it's getting worse. Then there's the crap weather, though I suppose we can't blame the government for that. I've had enough of it all so I've got my eye on some lovely little villas down in Spain. Dirt cheap, they are. I'm going to live out my twilight years in the sunshine."

Keith pondered what he could do or say. He knew Ted would never see those golden years unless he got him to see a doctor. There was only one thing for it. He was going to have to break his silence and warn him about his future. Was this the right thing to do? The bracelet suggested that it was, so he paused and thought carefully about what he was going to say.

"If you don't visit a doctor and get yourself sorted, you'll never make it to Spain. You'll be dead before the end of next year."

"Oh yeah?" said Ted defensively. "And what would you know about it?"

"Look, you are just going to have to trust me. Let's just say I have knowledge of the future."

"Really? Well, why aren't you writing the horoscopes, then? Maybe you could come up with something better than the drivel that idiot Gordon makes up."

"Look, just listen, will you? There's no easy way to explain this, so I'll just say it. I'm a time traveller from the future and I know with certainty that a month or two after you retire next year, you'll be admitted to hospital in agonising pain. While you're there, they'll discover you've got terminal stomach cancer and you'll be dead within three months. But that's all well over a year away. If you go to the doctor now, there's a chance they'll catch it early and be able to do something about it. What do you say?"

"I say, you spent too much time with Mad Harry yesterday and it's rubbed off on you. You're just as big a fantasist as he is."

"Look, I'm serious. Just go to the doctor. What harm can it do?"

"I'm tired of telling people this, but I don't have any time for doctors. From what I can see, the more people go to them, the more ill they become. They're like dodgy garages, telling you lots of things need fixing on your car when there's nothing wrong with it just to make more money out of you. I'm sorry but I just don't trust them."

"Your lack of trust is going to kill you. I've already seen it."

"Alright," said Ted. "If you can see the future, prove it."

He opened his desk and pulled out a Littlewoods Pools coupon for the following Saturday's games.

"Find me eight score draws on there and I'll believe you."

"It doesn't work like that," said Keith, frustrated. "I may have come from the future but I can't remember tiny details like that. If I gave you a pools coupon from this time last year, would you remember all the results? No."

"Ha, just I thought, this is all nonsense," said Ted. "Beryl from the canteen's put you up to this, hasn't she? She was going on at me last week about seeing a doctor. I don't know why people can't just mind their own business."

"No, it's nothing to do with Beryl. Now just hang on a minute, there are other things I know about the future, just give me a few moments and I'll show you," said Keith, wondering what information he could give Ted. If only he had made better use of the afternoon and evening after Elizabeth had given him the bracelet. What he should have done that day was go back home and cram every fact and detail about 1980 he could find on the internet into his head, in preparation. But he had decided to stay in the pub drinking all day instead. It had been a missed opportunity.

He grabbed a copy of the current day's paper from the desk. It was Friday 28th March 1980, and he started to flick through, searching for clues to future events. It had to be something significant and relatively imminent, not some vague prediction that wouldn't unfold for months. To convince Ted in time to help him, he needed something with more immediacy.

The news was dominated by a story about a disaster on an oil rig. That was of no use, it had already happened. What else was there? Some coverage of the ongoing hostage situation in Iran caught his eye. Now that could be useful. He recalled a specific event related to this crisis which was a siege at the Iranian Embassy in London. He couldn't remember exactly when but was reasonably confident it was going to happen soon.

Within the article about the hostages, he found a quote from President Carter, which gave him another idea. It was an election year in the USA and he remembered that the world had been surprised when the actor Ronald Reagan became president. This would occur later in the year and at this point, Reagan's nomination as the Republican candidate would not have been announced. This couldn't be far away either, so it was another piece of information he could share with Ted. And thinking about acting reminded him of *Dallas* again, so he threw in the news that JR would get shot soon for good measure.

Finally, he turned to the sports pages and spotted something he could use immediately. The Grand National was scheduled for tomorrow, and he skimmed the list of runners, hoping to recall the winner.

Luck was on his side. The name Ben Nevis stuck out like a sore thumb. It was one of the races that was etched in his memory. March 1980 had been exceptionally wet and everyone had been moaning about it raining for weeks on end. It was the same all over the country and the ground at Aintree was not far off being waterlogged. The race had been run in such bad conditions that only four horses had completed the course. Ben Nevis won at a big price and what's more, Keith had backed it all those years ago which presumably meant he was free to do so again, without disapproval from the bracelet.

What else did he have? His encyclopaedic knowledge of pop music? It was about time he made use of that. He went and found a copy of Wednesday's paper which was the one in which the new Top 40 was published every week after being revealed on the radio on Tuesday lunchtime. He cast his eye down the list, looking for songs that he knew were on their way up to the top.

The current chart topper was *Going Underground* by The Jam which had created somewhat of a sensation the previous week by going straight in at number one. Whilst this feat would be commonplace in later years, it was a rarity in these times and this was the first song for several years to achieve it.

However, his attention was drawn to the song at the very bottom of the chart. Propping up the rest with a new entry at number forty were Dexy's Midnight Runners with their classic anthem, *Geno*. In a few weeks, it would claim the number one spot but since the band were virtually unknown at this point, no one could have predicted it at this stage. This made it the perfect choice.

Armed with all this information, he went back to Ted and relayed it all to him. With a heavy scepticism, his colleague humoured him with the promise that he would go to the doctor if Keith's predictions came true. Now he just had to hope that the timeline stayed on track and events unfolded as they should. The pulsing green light on his wrist offered encouragement that he had done the right thing.

On Saturday, in the Mecca betting shop, he wrote out a bet for £50 to win on Ben Nevis. This action caused the bracelet on his wrist to glow a brighter red than it ever had before. It became so intense that the heat began to burn his wrist. He had wondered for a while what might happen if he knowingly broke the rules, and now he knew. He quickly altered the bet, crossing out the zero on the betting slip and changing it to a fiver, which was what he had originally bet on the horse. As soon as he did this, the bracelet cooled down, providing instant relief to his arm.

He wasn't pleased about this development at all. It reminded him of a science fiction film he had seen where enemies of the state were tagged with necklaces that would administer pain if they attempted to step out of a designated area. He had complied with all the other requests the bracelet had made, so why punish him just for seeking a little reward? It felt like he was being trained like a dog and he didn't appreciate it.

On the bright side, the horse won at odds of 40/1, earning him the equivalent of almost two weeks' wages. Jimmy was annoyed because his horse had fallen, despite Keith's advice to bet on Ben Nevis. Some people just couldn't be helped.

All this meant that Keith had made a successful start in his mission to save Ted, who was genuinely impressed with his tipping when he saw him back at work after the weekend, even if he wasn't ready to rush to the doctor just yet. He said it was just one prediction and brushed it off as a lucky guess but Keith wasn't perturbed. When all the other things he had told him started coming true, Ted would have no choice but to take him seriously. His life depended on it.

And it wasn't just Ted's life that was in the balance. With April on the way, Keith was about to face his most challenging task yet.

April 1980

"This is it, Keith!" exclaimed Jimmy, brimming with excitement as he bounded up to Keith's desk, rather like a dog bringing a stick back to its owner.

"What's it?" asked Keith, unaccustomed to seeing Jimmy so animated. "Did someone finally agree to go on a date with you?"

"Even better!" exclaimed Jimmy. "Bob Kelly's been rushed into hospital with suspected cirrhosis of the liver. And three girls are coming in today to audition for Page 3. With Bob indisposed, Jerry's asked me to handle it."

"I must say, Jimmy, that's rather tasteless, even by your standards," said Ted, chiming in from the next desk. "To celebrate another man's suffering just because it offers you an opportunity is despicable."

"Ted's right, you're out of order," said Keith, noticing the bracelet pulsing red. Was it merely disapproving of what Jimmy had said, or was it signalling something else entirely? No doubt he would find out soon enough.

"Yes, sorry," stammered Jimmy, his face reddening as he realised he had put his foot in it. Meanwhile, Ted commenced another of his customary coughing fits, severe enough to compel him to extinguish his half-smoked cigarette in the ashtray in front of him.

"That cough's getting worse, Ted," said Keith. "If you don't want to end up like Bob, you'd better get yourself down to the doctor. Remember our agreement? Ben Nevis, for starters."

"Just because you tipped the winner of the National doesn't mean you're Nostradamus," replied Ted. "I'm yet to see any of your other predictions materialise."

"What's this about?" asked Jimmy.

"Nothing for you to worry about," said Keith hurriedly, still keen to keep Jimmy in the dark. Changing the subject, he added, "Poor old Bob, eh? Life expectancy's not very good around here, is it? That's the third one hospitalised this year, all of them under sixty."

"Yes, we must send him a card or something," suggested Jimmy, trying to make amends for his earlier insensitivity. He genuinely liked Bob, though he had been irked by how he continually used his status as the paper's senior photographer to bag all the plum assignments. That included Page 3, which he considered his exclusive territory.

The bracelet was continuing to pulse red, reinforcing Keith's suspicion that something was amiss.

"What time are these girls coming in?" he asked.

"In about half an hour," said Jimmy.

"I think I'll tag along with you," said Keith. "You know, for moral support."

"Aye, aye," said Ted. "I know why you're going. For a bit of ornithology."

"Honestly, I'm not," said Keith. "It's just that Jimmy's not done this before, and I think he would benefit from my guidance."

"Is that what you're calling it?" said Ted. "Well, fill your boots, son. If you play your cards right, you might get lucky. Some of these girls are desperate to make it onto Page 3 and will do anything, and I mean anything to get picked. Why do you think old Bob never got married, eh? He never needed to if you know what I mean."

"Sounds good to me," said Jimmy eagerly.

"It sounds like exploitation to me," said Keith, and when he said that he meant it. When he had first arrived in 1980, these less enlightened times had initially seemed like a breath of fresh air compared to the moralistic, holier-than-thou world of 2019, where you could not say or do anything for fear of offending someone. However, after a few months in 1980, he was beginning to see that the good old days were not necessarily all they were cracked up to be. He was starting to wonder if he had been reminiscing about them before through rose-coloured spectacles.

The blatant sexism in the office had shocked him, despite having been part of it all those years before. He didn't remember it being this bad. The level of misogyny some of the men displayed in the office went far beyond mere banter. The way they spoke to the women who worked in the typesetting room, which was seemingly the highest job any woman could aspire to in the organisation, was outrageously condescending. It was also deemed acceptable to either pinch these women or slap them on the arse. Making lewd comments about various parts of their anatomy was also considered part of the fun.

Keith wasn't sure if this was true of all workplaces, or if it was particularly widespread in the world of journalism, but even he, considered a dinosaur in his era, found it incredibly uncomfortable. 1980 and 2019 were two extremes, and he couldn't say he cared much for either of them. The world of the past, of which he had held such treasured memories, was not the paradise he had believed it to be, whilst the future world had lurched too far in the opposite direction.

Why couldn't society find a happy medium? Where there was equality and opportunity for all, yet still room for a little gentle humour, celebrating people's differences, without prejudice or fear of a backlash? No, that would be too simple, wouldn't it? He sighed, realising he was wasting time on an insoluble problem and turned his attention back to Jimmy.

"What exactly does this process entail?" he asked.

"OK, so the girls come in and tell us a bit about themselves. Then we choose one, take some pictures, and then write a little blurb to go with it. Nothing too highbrow."

"You can say that again," said Keith, who had read some of the drivel that went alongside the pictures. "So what's the story with these three coming in today?"

"They are all new hopefuls, sent by agencies. We have our regulars but try and get at least one new girl each week. These are all unknowns and have never been in the papers before. This is their chance for a big break."

"And it's been left up to you to pick them?" asked Keith. "That seems like a lot of responsibility."

"I'm only doing it in Bob's absence because there's no one else to step into the breach at short notice. What normally happens is he recommends one to Jerry, who invariably goes along with it."

"And how does Bob reach this decision, exactly? By asking them to sleep with him and giving the job to whichever one complies?"

"I'm sure that's just a rumour," said Jimmy.

"Ha, you're so wet behind the ears," said Ted, who was still eavesdropping on the conversation.

"Well, perhaps it's just as well I'm coming along to keep an eye on things," said Keith. "We don't want any of these girls taking advantage of Jimmy's innocence, do we?"

"I don't mind," said Jimmy.

"Which is what I'm afraid of," said Keith, noticing the bracelet pulsing green as he spoke. It really did want him on this job. Why was that? he wondered.

When the time came, Keith followed Jimmy down the hallway towards the reception area. As they approached the glass doors, Keith could feel the power of the bracelet in his mind, preparing him for whatever lay ahead. Unlike before, there had been no dreams or premonitions. This time he was flying blind and would just have to hope he would know what do to when the time came.

That mystery was answered as soon as they entered the bright and spacious reception area. The girls were seated on a long leather sofa, chatting nervously amongst themselves. All three were strikingly beautiful, which didn't surprise him. They would not have got this far if they hadn't been, in an industry which valued physical appearance above all other attributes.

The first girl, who he could see from the name tags they had all been given, was named Emma, who had a rounded face framed by short blonde curls. Her figure was slim and elegant, accentuated by a figure-hugging dress that left little to the imagination. Despite her nervous laughter when they had come in, when she smiled she exuded an air of confidence that suggested she was no stranger to attention.

The second girl, Laura, had a more angular face with high cheekbones. Her black straight hair was straighter in sharp contrast to Emma's and of shoulder length. She seemed more nervous than Emma and didn't smile.

Beautiful as they both were, Keith's eyes were drawn like a magnet to the third girl, and with good reason. Unlike the other two, whom he had never seen before, he was now looking at the face of one of the most famous and tragic figures of the 1980s.

Rachel Summers was possibly the most famous Page 3 girl of all time. She had appeared in all the tabloids, starting at the tender age of eighteen, and had been a sensation, capturing the public's attention like no other before or since. Her beauty was undeniable, her long golden hair exquisite, and the body that would make her famous, sublime. But the thing that made her stand out, not just from the other two girls in the room, but every topless model who had ever graced the tabloids, was her piercing blue eyes. They exuded sexuality, whilst also suggesting a hint of vulnerability.

Everywhere she went, people adored her. Every man who caught her eye was bewitched by her, whilst all the women wanted to be her. She appeared so approachable, so real, the classic girl next door come good, and seemingly had the whole world at her feet. Then, in the space of a couple of short years, it all went horribly wrong.

Being the darling of the world might have seemed like a dream come true but as many rock stars had discovered, often at the cost of their own lives, it could weigh heavy on their shoulders. Rachel was ripe for exploitation by those out to make a quick buck. Soon every unscrupulous lowlife in London and beyond wanted a piece of her.

Once established, she could name her price for a photo shoot and she became very wealthy, very quickly. She could not go out of the house without being surrounded by the paparazzi and she attracted plenty of dubious attention too. Never one to shy away from a party, she found the champagne flowed freely, and it wasn't long until someone introduced her to drugs.

Some people could handle these things but others, with an addictive personality like Rachel, could not. Her cocaine habit developed fast and it wasn't long before even that was not enough. She began to make bad decisions, and having at one time stated she would never go full frontal, announced via the front pages that she would strip for the highest bidder. All the top-shelf magazines were falling over each other for the rights, with the bids running into the millions, as every week she became more and more addicted to drugs.

She did her best with excessive makeup to mask the effects of this on her appearance for a while, as her behaviour was becoming increasingly erratic. As she struggled, the world began to fall out of love with her, and the once adoring newspapers now began switching to stories where she was falling drunk out of taxi cabs and vomiting in the streets. And her latest addiction, judging by the kiss-and-tell stories starting to surface in the tabloids, was sex. By now, she had been lured into the porn industry which was booming, thanks to the growing prevalence of home video players.

The movies she was making weren't of the top-shelf, soft-porn variety which was about all you could legally buy in Britain at the time. This was hard-core porn, of the type most had to travel abroad to the Continent to obtain before attempting to smuggle it back through customs. And the content was shocking, as she was coerced into increasingly filthy and depraved practices.

Then one day in 1984, the world awoke to the news that she was dead, the victim of a heroin overdose at the age of just twenty-two. The papers went overboard with outpourings of emotion and grief, all trying to outdo each other to show they were the ones who had adored her the most. The fact that in the days leading up to her death, they had been systematically destroying what little self-esteem she had left was conveniently forgotten. And to his shame, Keith had been working at one of the worst offenders the whole time it was going on.

Looking at her now, so full of innocence and hope in reception, he felt like absolute shit. He was under no illusions about what had been done to her and whether directly or indirectly, simply by being part of this culture he had contributed to her downfall. If part of the bracelet's role had been to make him come back here and face the music for what he had done, then fair enough, he wasn't going to try to deny it or even justify it. He knew exactly what the people in his industry had done and he was as guilty as any of them.

As Keith looked at Rachel and the others, he could see now how shallow all of this was. Back in the 1980s, he had objectified these women just like everyone else. He wasn't excusing his behaviour. It would be easy to try to reason that he was young and driven by hormones or that it was the culture in the newsroom at the time and he was just following the example of everybody else. But those arguments held no weight. They were flimsy excuses at best.

Now, in his youthful body from which he was looking out at these young women with his middle-aged eyes, he had every reason to question the culture. Up until now it had just been little things that hadn't sat well with him, but the presence of Rachel had elevated things to a whole new level. Fleet Street, and the seedy world beyond into which she would soon be sucked, had scooped her up, bought her, sold her, and destroyed her. And it had all started right here, right now, at this very interview. He didn't need to look at the bracelet to know what he needed to do. Quite how he was going to do it was another matter.

Jimmy took the lead in the initial introductions and when the time came to take the first candidate into the meeting room, Keith interjected to ensure that one of the others was picked first. He needed time to think about what he was going to say to Rachel. In the meantime, he was going to do everything he could to prevent her being chosen. This wasn't going to be easy, as Rachel was so obviously the standout candidate.

The first to be interviewed was Emma, if you could call it an interview. Jimmy was completely unprepared for this, despite having had the same training as Keith.

Unable to drag his eyes away from the girl's cleavage, he mumbled a few lame questions about why she wanted to be on Page 3 before Keith took control of the situation.

Knowing the sort of thing that accompanied the pictures in the paper, Keith asked her about her background and hobbies, discovering she was a hairdresser who liked pop music and wanted to travel. It was hardly original stuff but keen to encourage her at Rachel's expense, he gushed enthusiastically at everything she said.

It was a similar story with Laura, who worked on the perfume counter at a department store. She also liked pop music and wanted to travel but didn't give a good impression. Keith thought she seemed a bit moody, but even so, he still gave her the same encouraging response. Then she left the room, paving the way for Rachel.

Keith had mulled over a few options while they had been interviewing Emma and Laura. How was he going to play this? He had come up with a few ideas but wasn't massively enthused by any of them. His first thought had been to behave like an absolute bastard and be the most misogynistic, horrible character possible. Make her see how awful people in this industry were and put her off that way.

But he dismissed this idea because it might not work and she was hardly likely to listen to any future advice from him if he made a bad first impression. So, instead, he decided he would be upfront with her and try to put her off by being honest about what she was potentially getting into. Jimmy was a likely obstacle but if he proved problematical he could always try to get Rachel on her own afterwards.

It seemed likely that Jimmy was going to be difficult. Despite Keith's attempts to big up the others, it had been obvious from the start how smitten Jimmy was with Rachel and that became even more apparent as soon as the interview began. The second he made eye contact with her Jimmy became transfixed, rendering him even more hopeless than he had been with the first two. It was up to Keith to take the lead in the conversation, one that he approached rather differently from the previous two.

She was quite different to the others. Her confidence showed not just in her poise but also in her choice of attire. Unlike the others, she hadn't worn a low-cut top showing off a mass of cleavage. She was dressed quite modestly, in a black T-shirt beneath a chequered red and black shirt, above a pair of jeans. She was wearing a trendy shoulder bag made of soft black leather with a long strap and a fold-over flap.

Despite this, there was no mistaking what she had come to advertise, even without thrusting her cleavage in their faces. The tight-fitting T-shirt showed off her figure quite amply, beneath which lay the pair of breasts that were soon destined to become the most photographed in the country.

Well, not if he had anything to do with it. After the initial introductions, Keith probed more deeply into her background, keen to find out every scrap of information he could about her. The more he knew, the more he might find something to assist in his efforts to dissuade her from the path she had followed before.

Her life was quite unlike that of the other girls, who had both come from urban working-class backgrounds. Rachel had attended a Christian school in a Home

Counties English village, where remarkably she was the daughter of the local vicar. In this sleepy environment she had grown up riding horses and taking piano lessons. Unlike Emma and Laura, who had left school at sixteen, Rachel was still in full-time education in the upper sixth where she was taking A-levels in biology, physics and chemistry.

"I've got to be honest," said Keith. "You don't fit the profile of the average Page 3 girl. It's only fair to warn you that this is a tough and cutthroat business. I'm not sure that a girl with your sheltered upbringing is going to be equipped to deal with it."

"And those two out there are? Just because they grew up in a city it doesn't mean they are streetwise. No offence to them, but they're as naïve as they come. And I have no illusions about what I'm getting into."

"I am sure you don't," said Keith, who couldn't help but be impressed by the young woman's bravado. "But I am more interested as to why."

"Oh, that's easy. My parents and teachers think I should go to university and study medicine, just because I'm top of the class. But I've had a lifetime of schooling and living in the sticks where nothing ever happens. I want excitement, I want fame and fortune and I want them now. Page 3 is my ticket to a glamorous life, full of adventure. I'm not going to get that at some stuffy academic institution."

"That life might not be all it's cracked up to be," said Keith. "I think you should consider your options carefully."

"Oh, believe me, I have," she said, attempting to fix Keith with the same mesmerising gaze that had already turned Jimmy's legs to jelly. He couldn't deny how compelling she was but he couldn't let that distract him.

"Well I think you're amazing, and you'd be my first choice any day of the week," said Jimmy unhelpfully.

"Thank you, Jimmy," she said, focusing her attention back on him. "Have you photographed many models before?"

"Oh, yes, lots," he said hurriedly, flattered that she seemed to be showing interest in him.

"Don't lie," said Keith to Jimmy, before turning back to Rachel. "He's never done this before."

"Well, we'll have to make your first time special, then, won't we, Jimmy?" said Rachel, not blinking once, and almost imperceptibly lowering her lower lip a fraction, just enough to let the tip of her tongue show.

"Right, I think that's enough for now," said Keith. "If you'd just like to wait outside with the others a moment, Rachel. Jimmy and I need to confer."

As soon as Rachel was out of earshot, Keith was ready to give Jimmy an earful, but his friend got in first.

"What the bloody hell are you playing at, Keith? She was clearly the best. She was as good as first past the post the moment she walked into the office."

"She's not right for this. Trust me."

"She was perfect. If we don't take her, one of the other tabloids will. She's the most beautiful girl I've ever seen. And she likes me, you heard what she said."

115

"She's not going to shag you, Jimmy. She's flattering you because she wants this job. Of course she's going to butter you up. And if you play into it, that makes you no better than Bob."

"That's rubbish. I'm not after her for that. But seriously, she's streets ahead of any of our regular girls. This could be the moment I've been waiting for to kick-start my career. Imagine if she does become a star. I would be the one that discovered her!"

"Look, I'm telling you, she's not right for this," said Keith, in frustration. "Just do as you're told and pick one of the others."

"No, Keith. I'm sick of you telling me what to do. I'm not your bloody lapdog. Just once, Lady Luck has cast her spell in my direction and not yours. Jerry made it quite clear the decision was mine and mine alone. I mean, what are you even doing here? This isn't your job. You're just trying to screw up mine."

"I'm sorry," said Keith, backtracking. He had gone too far. "But please, just back down on this one. I'll make it up to you, I promise. Say, how about I buy one of those Atari home videogame systems you keep going on about? My treat."

"Forget it. You're out of order. I'm choosing Rachel and that's that."

"And you're going to tell her now?"

"No, I can't do that. It needs to be done officially through the agency. Besides, if I tell her out there I'll have to see the others being disappointed, won't I?"

"You're such a coward. I guess we'd better let them go, then. I mean, there's no point in them hanging around in reception if there's nothing else for them to do, is there? When are you going to call the agency?"

"After lunch. I just need to run it by Jerry first."

"Right, well we'd better see them out, then," said Keith, and they returned to reception, where Jimmy thanked them and said they would be in touch.

As he turned back to the office, Keith took his leave of Jimmy.

"Listen, mate, you head back to the office, and I'll catch you up. I've just got to pop out for something."

Walking quickly across reception, Keith was away and gone before Jimmy could ask any further questions. He had one chance left, and one chance only, and that was to convince Rachel to turn down the offer. Whatever he was going to do, he had to act swiftly for her sake, or her future was going to be a short one.

He needed to get outside quickly because she would soon disappear into the crowd on the busy street. Exiting the building, he ran between the pillars, and past the flowerbeds which were replete with daffodils, turning their heads towards the warm spring sunshine. Out on the street, he was relieved to see she was just a few yards ahead and not walking with the others.

"Rachel!" he called, hoping she would be receptive to his unexpected reappearance. "Can I talk to you? How about we go and grab a bite of lunch?"

Rachel looked surprised. She stopped and looked him up and down, trying to size up what he might want.

"Are you propositioning me, in return for getting me in the paper?" she asked. "Because they tried that at your rivals down the road, after which I told them I'd take my business elsewhere. I'm not selling myself for anyone."

"Isn't that exactly what you are doing?" replied Keith. "As soon as you decided you wanted to splash yourself all over Page 3?"

"But no one's getting their hands on me personally, are they? That's the appeal. It's a fantasy that everyone who opens the paper can dream of but none of them can have. Only I get to choose who can touch me, and when I do, no money or favours will be changing hands."

"I promise you, my intentions are honourable," he insisted. "I've just got a few more questions I didn't have time for in the meeting. Let's go and grab a drink and have a chat. It's all on me. We journalists get a very generous expense account."

"So you're putting me on your expenses?" she said, looking him straight in the eye once again, seemingly weighing him up to try to ascertain the true nature of his intentions.

"Sure, why not? If the paper's happy to pay for our drinks, who are we to argue?"

"Over there?" she suggested, pointing towards a historic-looking pub called Ye Olde Cheshire Cheese, just along the street.

"No, not there," said Keith, knowing that the pub in question was a favourite with his colleagues and they would never get any privacy if they went there. "Somewhere quieter."

Keith led her out of Fleet Street to a pub a couple of hundred yards away where he hoped they would be away from prying eyes. As they entered the small pub, frequented more by tourists than locals, he considered his approach carefully. How could he explain to her that the path she was set on would lead to a dark and painful future? What alternatives could he offer that would appeal more than the fame and fortune she so obviously craved?

"What are you having?" he asked at the bar.

"Double vodka – neat," she replied.

"Wow, you don't mess about, do you?" he replied. "It's barely gone noon."

"Like you said, the paper's paying," she said, as he ordered her drink and a pint of lager for himself. As soon as they were seated in a quiet corner, she pulled out a packet of Benson & Hedges and lit up, offering one to Keith at the same time. He duly obliged, despite his preference for Marlboro.

"Right then," she began, sipping at her vodka. "What's this all about?"

"Rachel," he began with trepidation. "I can see that you are an incredibly confident and ambitious young woman and that's wonderful. But I'm here to tell you that you are embarking on an incredibly dangerous path, and one that's going to lead you into a world of misery."

Rachel listened intently, her eyes never leaving his, as she took a deep draw on her cigarette, pursed her lips slightly and with a carefully controlled motion released the smoke in a series of short puffs. With each exhalation, a perfect ring of smoke emerged, expanded and floated slowly away.

"I want you to think seriously about taking a different road," Keith continued. "One where you can fulfil your potential for the benefit of others, without going down the rocky road of fame which has led so many to their deaths. Look at what happened to Janis Joplin, Jimi Hendrix, and Jim Morrison. Do you want to end up like them?"

"Those were all rock stars," replied Rachel. "That's a career notorious for drug abuse. I've never heard of anything like that happening to a Page 3 girl."

"That doesn't mean it doesn't," said Keith. "You've no idea what it's like out there. It's a tough dog-eat-dog world, where only the strongest survive. And I don't think you're strong enough."

"No offence, Keith, but quite honestly you don't know anything about me. You just met me today. Now, I can't see for the life of me what your motivation is for bringing me in here and trying to put me off something I've got my heart set on but let me tell you – I don't appreciate it."

"But why? I mean, look at your pedigree. A vicar's daughter with a wholesome, rural upbringing. You don't exactly fit the mould."

"Which is precisely why I want to do this! Do you know how boring it was growing up in that village? Nothing ever happened. When the highlight of the year was the annual fete where the biggest claim to fame was which old git could grow the biggest marrow, you can hardly blame me for wanting to get out."

She downed the remainder of her vodka and handed him the glass.

"Same again, please," she said, stubbing out her cigarette and immediately lighting another.

120

He didn't feel like he was getting very far but when he glanced at the bracelet he could see it was pulsing green, which suggested he was doing the right thing. He just needed to try harder. Back at the table, he renewed his efforts.

"Is that why you're doing this, then? As a backlash against your upbringing? Because that's hardly a rational reason for a career choice."

"Maybe not, but it's good enough for me."

"Is it, though? How long do you think that fame will last? Yes, you may have the looks and the body, but those things fade. What will you be doing when you're fifty? And it's not like you haven't got alternatives. You said earlier, that you're a straight-A student with a talent for science. You could walk into any university and do a degree in medicine, or any other field. Something that would set you up for life, and one that's not dependent on your body to earn you a living."

As he said the last few words he waved a hand towards her breasts to emphasise his point.

"I won't need to earn a living when I'm fifty. I'll be so rich I'll never need to earn another penny again."

Keith wasn't getting through to her. He was going to have to play his trump card.

"You won't need any money when you're fifty, because you'll be in your grave. Continue down the path you're on and you'll be dead within five years."

"Oh, come on!" she exclaimed. "Where do you get off on making such wild predictions? Next, you'll be telling me you can see into the future."

"As a matter of fact, I can. You're going to die in 1984 of a heroin overdose after years of substance abuse, brought on by the pressures of fame."

"I'm sorry, but that's nonsense," she said. "For a start, I've never been near drugs in my life. I've never even seen drugs. I don't even know what they look like."

"Believe me, once you get started in this industry you will. You say you want fame and fortune? That means high-class parties, with pop stars, actors and more."

"Bring it on."

"And what do you think goes on at those parties? You'll be offered a line before you know it, and you won't want to turn it down, not if you don't want to look like a party pooper in front of all those famous people."

"I'm sorry, but what makes you think I'm not strong enough to refuse?"

"You've got an addictive personality. I mean, look at you now. We've been here, what, twenty minutes and you've already knocked back two double vodkas and you're on your third cigarette. You're eighteen years old yet you're drinking and smoking like an old pro."

"I'm not doing anything illegal. Why shouldn't I enjoy myself?"

"But could you give it up? If I asked you to stop smoking here and now, would you be able to?"

"Why would I want to? Smoking helps me keep my weight down. And vodka's the best drink for doing the same."

"I didn't ask if you wanted to, I asked if you could. Or are you addicted already? Because addiction and you go hand in hand and it's going to be the death of you."

"According to you and your fantasies about a fictional future, of which you claim to have knowledge. But it hasn't happened yet, so what makes you think I'm destined to go down that road?"

"Because I've already seen it."

"How? Come on, if you're going to make such bold claims, back them up. You can see the future, right?"

"That's just the thing, I can't."

"Can't what, back them up or see the future? I think you're making this whole thing up."

"Yes, but why?" asked Keith. "What's in it for me?"

"I don't know, maybe you're some sick fantasist who gets off on this sort of crap. If you can see the future you need to prove it. Here and now. Describe the next person who is going to walk in the front door."

"It doesn't work like that."

"Of course it doesn't. You're full of shit."

"Look, I can tell you stuff about the future but not things that are going to happen in the next few minutes. I'm talking about things that are going to happen in the next few months. I've already done it with a guy I work with at the paper. He was facing death in less than two years because he wouldn't go to the doctor. But I've told him stuff no one could possibly know. Within a month or two, he'll have no choice but to believe me."

"I don't have a month or two. I need to make my decision today."

123

"You're right, you do, and you need to make the right one. Because your very life depends on it."

"You're going to have to come up with something a lot better than that. I want a bloody good explanation as to how you claim to know so much about my future. And it had better be good because if it isn't, I'm straight on the phone to my agent when I get back to take the job, which I guarantee Jimmy's going to offer me."

"Very well," said Keith, embarking on the same lengthy account that he had given Ted, complete with predictions, as well as a detailed explanation of Rachel's spectacular slide into depravity and eventual death.

"What do you think?" he said at the end.

Rachel had a pensive look on her face as she contemplated his words. The allure of the career she had been so sure about before today was still strong but there was more than a glimmer of doubt in her eyes.

"It sounds like total fantasy," she said, "but then I'm still asking myself, what could be in it for you? If you'd wanted to chat me up, you could have found far more conventional ways of doing it. I might even have responded – you're a good-looking fella with bags of charisma. But coming out with this sort of stuff would cause most women to run a mile, and you must know that. So I can only conclude that you truly believe what you're telling me which leaves two possibilities. Either you're mentally ill or it's true."

"It is true," said Keith. "Now listen, I've got a suggestion. Time is on your side. I'm not sure if it's on mine, but that's another story. This is what I suggest you do. Finish your A-levels. Apply to university and study medicine. Who knows, you could be the person who one day discovers the cure for cancer. Isn't that more fulfilling than having dirty old men perving over your boobs in the paper?"

"I suppose when you put it like that…"

"Just give it six months. Watch my predictions come true. And if they don't, and you conclude it's all bullshit, then there's nothing to stop you from going back down the modelling route. Today isn't your one and only shot at fame. If you came back to the papers this time next year and tried again, they'd still be falling over themselves to bid for you."

"Bid for me?"

"Yes, because that's all you are to them. A commodity to be bought and sold to make them even richer than they already are. You're better than that, and you know it."

"OK," she said, still looking uncertain. "I need to think about this."

"I know you'll make the right choice," said Keith. "And will you do something for me? Come and look me up before the end of the year and let me know how things turned out."

"I haven't made my decision yet," she said, getting to her feet and placing her cigarettes back into her leather bag. "But I will think about it, I promise."

And with that she was gone, leaving Keith to finish his pint. Had he done enough? The bracelet seemed to think so.

Later that afternoon, a furious Jimmy came over to his desk, eyes blazing with vitriol. He had never seen him so cross.

"What the hell did you say to her, Keith?"

"Who?" asked Keith, feigning innocence, even though he knew Jimmy had rumbled him.

"Rachel!" he said. "She's turned us down. So now I've got to give it to one of the others instead."

"So where's the problem?"

"I wanted her. She was something special. You must have been able to see that."

"I did. Perhaps she just got cold feet. It happens, you know. It may all seem very glamorous but when the reality of getting their knockers out for the public kicks in, some of these girls probably bottle it."

"You said something to her. I know you did. Gordon said he saw the two of you walking down Fleet Street together."

"Gordon should keep his nose out of other people's business. Anyway, it's all done and dusted now. Give the job to Emma instead. She was alright."

"Fine," said Jimmy, storming off before adding, "but I'm not happy about it."

He might not have been happy about it, but Keith was. It seemed he had successfully negotiated another mission and saved a life in the process. What next?

May 1980

"What's that?" asked Jimmy, intrigued by the strange colourful object that Keith was fiddling with as they sat on the sofa on a sunny bank holiday Monday, the one that fell during the last week of May.

"It's a Rubik's Cube," said Keith. "Just been launched. This is going to be the must-have toy of 1980."

Jimmy watched fascinated as Keith expertly manipulated the faces of the cube in his hands, his skill in solving it evident. His fingers moved with precision as the puzzle's faces twisted and turned under his control, aligning themselves into orderly patterns with each calculated move. It was as if he had been playing with the thing for years, which indeed he had. He had mastered this back in the eighties and in a couple of short minutes, he had all the faces neatly lined up with the correct colours.

"Wow!" said Jimmy. "That was quick."

"The world record is five seconds or something ridiculous like that," said Keith, not remembering the exact number only that it was something implausibly short. "Now you have a try."

He shuffled it back up and handed it over, watching with amusement as Jimmy, huffing with frustration, struggled to get to grips with the cube.

"This is hopeless," he said after a couple of minutes. "Shall we go to the pub?"

"I told you, we can't go to the pub until after *Dallas*. Tonight's the night JR gets shot, and I want to watch it."

127

"Yes, so you can be proved right," replied Jimmy in an annoyed tone, brought on by Keith's predictions always coming true. "Anyway, I don't think you're as clever as you're making out. Everyone already knows he's going to get shot. It was shown in America several weeks ago and the BBC have been hyping it up for ages too. Terry Wogan talks about nothing else."

"Yes, but I want to figure out who did it," said Keith, who still couldn't remember but hoped that the episode would bring it all back.

"Fine, well can we go to the pub as soon as it's finished? It is a bank holiday, after all, and decent weather for once. We're missing out on all the fun."

"It finishes at nine, there will be plenty of time."

After the show, Jimmy was convinced he knew the identity of the shooter.

"It was obviously Sue Ellen," he confidently declared. "She had a gun."

"Yes, which makes it too obvious," said Keith, who did now have a strong inkling who was responsible. "You know, I'm pretty sure it was her sister."

"Well, quite honestly, I don't care. There are two pints of Carling Black Label with our names on them in The George & Dragon and I want to get down there. Oh, by the way, do you want to go and see *The Empire Strikes Back* tomorrow night?"

"Nah, I've seen it before."

"How can you have seen it before? The premiere was only the other night and you haven't been anywhere without me since then."

"I'm telling you I have. And I'll prove it. Darth Vader is Luke Skywalker's father."

"Bollocks."

"You'll see. Now, let's get going, if we're going," replied Keith, and with that they headed off to the pub.

The following day, all the talk in the office was of the shooting of JR. Keith, not shy in offering his opinion on the subject, was given the task of writing a double-page feature all about it. Just as he had predicted, the country was going *Dallas* crazy, and on his way to the pub for lunch, he saw a guy wearing a T-shirt with the logo 'I shot JR' emblazoned upon it.

It was a craze that was set to run and run because the show's fans were going to have to wait until the start of the show's fourth season in the autumn to find out whodunit.

One employee notable by his absence was Ted, who did not show up in the office until teatime. When he did, he headed straight over to Keith, who was busy reading through a biography of the actor Larry Hagman.

"Keith, my boy!" said Ted loudly and full of the joys of spring as he grabbed his hand and began pumping it enthusiastically. "I cannot thank you enough! Can you guess where I have been?"

"You went to the doctor, finally?" asked Keith, looking around nervously, to see if Ted's uncharacteristic lively demeanour had attracted the attention of anyone nearby.

"Three weeks ago," said Ted. "The day after the Iranian Embassy siege and the same week that Dexy's Midnight Runners went to number one. Plus, it's been looking increasingly likely Reagan's going to get the Republican nomination. So I decided to bite the bullet and go."

"I don't understand," said Keith. "Why didn't you say anything?"

"Because then you would have been badgering me for weeks wanting to know what was going on. You know what I'm like about medical stuff. I thought I would keep it to myself until I knew I was going to be alright."

"And are you?"

"Yes. The doctor sent me for some tests at the hospital. I can't believe how quickly they got me in."

"And did they find anything?"

"Yes, but they've caught it early. I've got to have some treatment, but they say after that I'll be fine. That's where I was today, getting the results and having a consultation about what happens next. And one thing they did tell me was that if I hadn't got myself checked out, given another year or so it could have been a very different story. I don't know how you became blessed with the gift to see the future, but I can't express how grateful I am."

"Listen, Ted, can you do me a favour?" asked Keith, keeping his voice low, all too aware that they were surrounded by inquisitive journalists. They were the last people he wanted to take an interest in his special powers.

"Anything, son. I'm forever in your debt."

"Can you keep quiet about it? I mean, I don't want to attract unwelcome attention."

"Well, I already told the oncologist at the hospital about you but I don't think he believed me."

"Good, well let's keep it that way," said Keith, as Ted reached into his desk for his trusty bottle of Scotch.

"Will you have a drink with me to celebrate?"

"I'm surprised they didn't tell you to cut down on that stuff," said Keith.

"I didn't give them the opportunity. I told them I didn't drink. That way they couldn't tell me to stop. I'm not daft!"

"You're a sly old bugger, I'll give you that," said Keith, as the bracelet pulsed green to confirm another job well done. If Ted still ended up drinking himself to death in some other way, at least he had given him a few more years.

He was feeling pretty pleased with himself right now. Doing good deeds wasn't something he had been renowned for before his trip back in time. But he had to admit, it gave him a warm feeling, and not in the fake way that he was used to seeing from the virtue-signalling loons of the twenty-first century. He hated the way they jumped on every bandwagon going, putting various flags and symbols on their social media profiles and shouting from the rooftops about how caring they were.

Unlike them, he felt like he had made a genuine difference now to at least three people's lives, and not for any self-serving reasons of his own. He genuinely liked Robin, Rachel, and Ted, and could see the merit now in what he was doing. He had questioned the motives of whoever had invented the bracelet to begin with but now he was beginning to understand its importance.

After sharing an illicit drink with Ted, Keith turned his attention to the day's business. With the football season concluded, one of the main sports writers had taken a week's leave before heading off to cover England's performance at the European Championships. That meant his team were short-staffed, so Keith, who was very much still one of the office juniors, had been put onto sport for the week.

He picked up Tuesday's paper and turned to the back, to see what was going on. His eyes were immediately drawn to the headline on the back page.

Multimillionaire businessman to buy Chelsea.

That was interesting. What was that all about? He remembered Roman Abramovich buying Chelsea and investing a fortune that took them to the Premier League title but that was decades later. Right now, Chelsea FC was in the doldrums, stuck in the second division and going backwards.

What was also interesting was that as he read through the article, the bracelet began pulsing red. Was something going on here that he needed to get involved with?

The story was all about an incredibly wealthy property developer by the name of James Colby. He had made his fortune from redeveloping areas of London that had been bombed out in the Second World War. The article explained that he now wanted to invest some of his fortune in restoring his beloved football club to its former glories.

Something about the article didn't ring true, and what's more, he had never heard of this character. Surely if this man had bought Chelsea, he would at least have known his name, even if football wasn't Keith's thing.

Curious, he asked Ted if he knew anything about it.

"First I've heard of it," said Ted. "But it sounds a bit iffy to me."

"In what way?"

"Well, who invests in football? There's no money in it. Look at all those lower-division clubs, struggling to make ends meet. Any businessman worth his salt would steer well clear."

What Ted was saying was true about the state of the game at this time. Attendances were falling for many reasons, rampant hooliganism being just one of them. Football was a long way from the multi-million money spinner it would later become on the back of SKY TV money and the formation of the Premier League. But even so, there were signs of what was to come, most notably in the transfer fees paid for star players.

"What about Trevor Francis?" said Keith, referring to the player who had made history the previous year when sold to Nottingham Forest for a landmark fee. "The first million-pound football player."

"Ridiculous," said Ted. "It's an obscene sum."

It was, but it was dwarfed by the players of forty years later who were changing hands for figures in the hundreds of millions.

"You don't think he'll buy them, then?"

"No, it's all bullshit. I reckon it's just a blown-up story to keep football on the back pages while it's out of season. Our circulation always drops in the summer, so we've got to do something to keep the punters interested."

"And what about this James Colby character? Know anything about him?"

"Only what's in the paper. David wrote that article at the weekend before he went off on holiday."

"Hmmm. Well, I reckon there's something dodgy about this."

"Your intuition again?" asked Ted, raising his eyebrows knowingly.

"Not exactly," said Keith, though the red jewel on the bracelet was certainly hinting that way.

Overnight, he got the whole story. Just as with his Winter Olympic dream, he saw a potential alternate future, one in which the mysterious James Colby did indeed take control of Chelsea. He picked them up for a rock-bottom price, pledging to turn them into world-beaters within five years. Most of the fans welcomed him to Stamford Bridge with hopes that better times were ahead but there were a few who expressed doubts. They were right to be sceptical.

His first act as chairman was to sack the club's manager, none other than England's World Cup hat trick hero, Geoff Hurst, who was practically a national treasure. In his place, Colby brought in an unemployed fourth-division manager whose only notable 'achievement' was to have succeeded in getting any club he had ever been in charge of relegated.

Solid players were sold off at bargain basement prices and replaced by thirty-five-year-old glamour purchases – former stars, long past their best, on massive salaries. The club plummeted in the table and within two years suffered two more relegations, ending up in the fourth division by 1982. Increasingly disgruntled fans staged protests, sit-ins, pitch invasions and there was even a riot but all this did was hasten the demise.

Amid allegations of illegal and immoral practices, the club collapsed with massive debts and simply ceased to exist. When it was declared bankrupt, the assets were transferred to a property company, in which Colby just happened to be a major shareholder. After five years, far from being league champions, the prime land in West London where Chelsea had once played now became the construction site for a rapidly growing skyscraper.

As for the allegations and accusations, none of them could be proved. It was strongly suspected that Colby had illegally siphoned off millions from the club but it seemed to be untraceable. If he had left any trail behind him, it was very well hidden and this was not the limit of his ambitions by any means. In his dream, Keith foresaw a future where Colby had become the richest man in Britain, riding roughshod over its cultural heritage, ripping up whatever the hell he liked to expand his empire. It appeared that nobody was able to stop him, not councillors, not MPs, and not journalists. With the amount of money he had he was able to buy whatever, and whoever, he wanted.

It was blindingly obvious in the morning that he needed to stop this. What he wasn't sure was how he was going to go about it. James Colby was a man who wasn't easy to investigate. He had seen in his detailed dream how others had tried to catch him out and take him down over the years, but he was as slippery as they come. There were a couple of things he had on his side. This was still relatively early in Colby's career and he did not at this stage command the level of power he would in later years. And crucially, no one else who had tried to take him down had possessed the benefit of the bracelet. It had guided him before and it could help him again.

At the office, he ran his concerns past his usual confidante, Ted. However, he didn't get the reaction he had hoped for when he related the tale of Chelsea's demise.

"Good. I fucking hate Chelsea," said Ted, rubbing his hands with glee.

"That's not the point," said Keith, recalling that Ted was a Spurs fan. "The point is that this fellow thinks he can steamroller over everyone and everything in his pursuit of world domination, and we've got to stop him."

"And how do you propose to do that?"

"I was hoping you might be able to offer some advice. I mean, just imagine if I can expose this bloke. That would be a major scoop for the paper."

"It's not me you've got to convince. It's Jerry."

So Keith went to Jerry, careful not to reveal anything he knew about the future. He confined himself to expressing his concerns over Colby and requesting permission to spend some time digging into his past.

Jerry reluctantly agreed to let him spend a couple of hours on it, but no more. He was not convinced there would be anything to find.

A couple of hours wasn't much time, using the laborious processes of tracking down information in the early 1980s. With no Google to hand, Keith paid a visit to the newspaper's archives in the basement of the building. It was a dusty old place which was rumoured to be infested with rats, though Keith had never seen any. There were plenty of cobwebs though, giving the place an air of neglect, and being below ground, no windows. Here, decades of material both from their newspaper and all the other dailies was stored on an ancient system called microfiche.

Keith had spent many an hour down here in his early days on the paper and had to admit, the system was efficient for its time. It worked by miniaturising the pages of the newspapers onto small rectangular sheets that resembled film negatives. Each sheet was about the size of a postcard and contained multiple pages of content organised in a grid pattern. To view the information, it was necessary to place the sheets under a reader, which worked like a cross between an overhead projector, to illuminate the information, and a giant magnifying glass to restore the text to a readable size.

It would be like looking for a needle in a haystack to go through this stuff without an index, but fortunately everything was catalogued in precise detail. It was as good as any encyclopaedia, directing Keith to the relevant sheets and grid location upon them that he needed. These were held in rows and rows of dull grey filing cabinets. He located the earliest article he could find about Colby, from 1968, and thus began his investigation.

Over the next couple of hours, the evidence he amassed was inconclusive but certainly suspicious. Colby, or companies he had a stake in, had been involved in quite a few acquisitions of a questionable nature over the years. However, on no occasion was there any accusation of wrongdoing. They were just coincidences, for example, a farmer who was standing in the way of the building of a new industrial estate whose farmhouse had burnt down under mysterious circumstances.

In another case, the building of a housing estate had led to the extinction of a rare type of butterfly, yet mysteriously the environmental report that would have prevented this had not come to light until it was already too late. In another, a shopping centre was green-lighted at the expense of a Grade 2 listed building, where again, proper procedures were not followed. This was also put down to administrative error.

These were just a few examples, but nothing was damning or incriminating that could be pinned on Colby. It was what the police might refer to as circumstantial evidence but with what he already knew, Keith was convinced that these convenient errors were not just cock-ups.

It wasn't enough for Jerry, who took the same line that the police would. It didn't help that he was a Chelsea fan and all for the proposal. So, if Keith was going to take this further he was going to have to do it without the paper's support.

Once again, he turned to Ted, hoping to dip into the veteran journalist's extensive experience.

"Come on, Ted. You were a war correspondent and behind enemy lines at one point. You must know all about this sort of thing."

"What I did was probably easier than the sort of corporate espionage you're talking about."

"How can it have been? You were fighting Nazi Germany, for heaven's sake."

"Yes, but I had the full support of the British Intelligence Services behind me. What have you got?"

"Nothing, but look, I'm not going behind enemy lines with the risk of being shot, am I? I just want to get into his office. He must have something incriminating in there."

"I'm sure he has. What's your plan, waltz in and ask if you can have a look around? Good luck with that."

"Of course not. I don't know what my plan is. That's why I'm asking you. And you did say you owed me a favour, remember?"

"I did," said Ted. "But it's not going to be easy. Even if you did get in there undetected, I doubt anything incriminating will just be lying around for anyone to see. It will be tightly locked away."

"Yeah, that's what I was worried about," said Keith, slumping back in his seat and putting his hands behind his head as he wondered what he could do next. Then Ted threw him a lifeline.

"There is someone that owes me a favour who may be able to help. Perhaps it's time I called in Locksmith Larry."

139

"Locksmith Larry?" said Keith, raising his voice incredulously. "Who's that? He sounds like a character off *Minder*."

"Keep your voice down," said Ted. It was now his turn to look around to check no one was eavesdropping. Then he added, very quietly, "You must not breathe a word of this to anyone. Not only is what I am going to suggest potentially dangerous, but it's also highly illegal. I mean career-ending, probable prison time level of illegal. If you want to back out, now would be the time."

Keith pondered this, looking to the bracelet for an opinion, and it was glowing green. Experience had taught him that if the bracelet approved, he was probably on safe ground, however dangerous Ted claimed this was going to be. If he trusted the bracelet, he would have nothing to fear.

"I'm in," he said confidently.

June 1980

"I'm impressed," said Keith through the balaclava he wore, as Locksmith Larry expertly manipulated the safe's dial.

The office the two of them had broken into was dimly lit, and Keith was shining a torch on the dial of the sturdy metal safe, as Larry worked his magic. As he nervously struggled to keep the beam steady, he became aware that he was breathing heavily as if he had been working out, but it was all down to the adrenalin rush coming from the danger of their situation. Despite one or two dubious practices during his journalistic career, Keith had never been involved in anything like this before and the gravity of the situation weighed heavily on his shoulders.

"You should be," replied Larry, his focus unwavering on the task in front of him. "If they gave out prizes for this sort of thing, I'd be a gold medallist, many times over."

He wasn't exaggerating. Locksmith Larry was a unique talent. He had been a crucial asset in numerous covert operations during the war when his exceptional skills as a safecracker enabled him to obtain key documents from behind enemy lines. These had contained invaluable intelligence that had greatly assisted with the war effort. In the post-war years, he had turned to a life of crime. Applying his talents to the wrong side of the law, he had earned the respect of many underworld figures who sought his services.

What set Larry apart from others of his ilk was his unblemished record. Despite facing suspicion from authorities on countless occasions, he had always managed to elude them. The same could not be said of most of his peers who had invariably ended up in Wormwood Scrubs at some point. By now, he was living comfortably and semi-retired from his illegal activities but he had never forgotten the debt he owed to Ted, who had saved his life during a perilous encounter with the Nazis in occupied France. The two men had kept in touch ever since, occasionally sharing information which helped both in their respective professions.

Ordinarily Larry would expect to be well compensated for this sort of work, but for Ted, it was on the house. Plus, he was enjoying the challenge. As the years passed, security had become increasingly sophisticated but it had always been his proud boast that the lock hadn't been designed yet that he couldn't break.

As the dial clicked into place, Larry's experienced hands turned it smoothly to the next number. The safe was an imposing steel fortress with one of the most advanced designs of combination lock available at the time. The technology of 1980 meant that this was no digital lock; it relied on a complex system of tumblers and precise combinations, and a lesser man would have declared it to be impenetrable.

Keith watched in fascination as Larry's gloved fingers worked with the precision of a doctor performing complex surgery. The whole process took him less than five minutes, and with a final turn, there was a subtle, almost imperceptible click.

"Open sesame," said Larry, pulling the heavy door open, revealing a cache of confidential files. It was exactly what Keith had hoped to find.

It had been over a week since Ted had enlisted Larry's help, and shortly afterwards the three of them had met up in a pub. Unlike Ted, Larry was a Chelsea fan and extremely interested in what Keith had to say. Over several large Scotches, they discussed plans and how to implement them. The most important part, Larry had explained, was not to rush into things. Their preparations had to be meticulous if the plan was to be watertight.

First they had staked out the building, a six-storey office block in the West End, using the old trick of dressing up as plumbers to attend to a fictitious problem. Larry was an old hand at this and knew exactly the right things to say to get past security.

They did this late in the day when many of the workers were already heading home. This gave them unsupervised access to check out the layout of the building, including the location of Colby's office. By the time they left, well into the evening, they had also established the routine of the overnight security staff. There was just one guard, who patrolled the building every hour. It was surprisingly lax considering their target's reputation, but as Keith had previously surmised, it was early days in Colby's career. In his visions of the target's later life, he had seen him in far grander circumstances where he was permanently protected by a formidable security team. It couldn't be more clear. He needed nipping in the bud now.

They returned after dark on a Saturday evening when the office was closed for the weekend. They broke in via a fire escape at the back of the building that Larry had identified on their previous visit as a type he could open without triggering any alarms. While they knew that the security guard had primitive CCTV covering the entrances and exits, they also knew that he spent around twenty minutes out of every hour patrolling the building. It was a fixed routine, so all they needed to do was time their entry accordingly. To be doubly sure, they watched the windows from outside. When lights started going on and off around the building, they knew that was when he was on patrol.

Safely inside, they made their way to Colby's office where they knew they had just under an hour to find what they had come for. Once the safe was open, they pored over the incriminating documents looking for evidence. It didn't take long to find. Larry's eyes were drawn to a file marked "Project Blue," a reference to Chelsea's colours and nickname, and he flicked it open as Keith passed his torch over it.

"It's all here," said Keith, rifling through with his thinly gloved fingers, finding details not only of the plan but also several letters from various interested stakeholders. Of these, the most incriminating was a letter guaranteeing planning permission from a prominent council official in return for a substantial cash payment. "There's enough here to have him hung, drawn and quartered several times over."

"We've got less than half an hour before that security guard checks this floor again," said Larry. "You realise we can't take any of this stuff with us, don't you? That would be theft. We need to take copies of everything we need and leave this intact exactly as we found it. Then there is no evidence we were ever here."

"Pity," said Keith. "As I wonder what else he's got in all those other files."

"Oh, I'm sure that will all come out later if we get him for this," said Larry, taking the opportunity to sit down at Colby's desk. "Bloody hell, this is tiring. I'm getting too old for this."

Keith shone the torch briefly towards him, noting the wet patch on the balaclava above his eyes which could only have been sweat on this warm summer night. Larry must have been pushing seventy, was carrying a lot of weight and was breathing even more heavily than he was. He couldn't see his face, but his posture leaning back in the desk suggested he was knackered. For one horrible moment, Keith worried that his companion might expire. The sooner they got out of there, the better.

"Right, well, look, there's a Xerox machine over there. We can use that."

"You must be joking," said Larry. "You work in a newsroom, you must know how much noise those things make. That's when they even work properly. I've got a much better idea."

He leaned forward and reached down to the floor for the bag of tricks he had brought along, producing what looked like a small compact camera.

"A camera?" asked Keith. "But it will be too dark in here, surely?"

"My, my, you are new to all this, aren't you? No, this is a microfilm camera. The latest model, as used by the intelligence services. This is the sort of thing Q might

145

give Bond when he goes out on a mission. I can copy all these documents, and they'll be reduced to microfilm. Then you blow them up later."

"Like the microfiche we use in the office?"

"Exactly like that," replied Larry. "Now, you pass me the documents, one at a time, and I'll capture them."

The whole operation was over in less than fifteen minutes, giving them ample time to tidy up and leave the office exactly as they had found it.

"Not a trace," said Keith, flashing the torch around one last time to check.

"That security guard should be leaving his desk right about now. Provided we follow the route back out we planned earlier, we should comfortably avoid him."

They successfully made their way back out via the fire escape, disposed of their balaclavas and gloves, and made their way back to the busy city streets. Jimmy was annoyed when Keith returned to the flat after midnight, complaining that he had ruined their Saturday evening by not coming back after he had supposedly nipped out to the shops just before teatime. Keith brushed this off by claiming he had spent the evening in bed with some woman he had hit it off with at the shops, gave a completely insincere apology, and then went straight to bed.

On Monday morning he met Larry again, who had now developed and blown up the documents. Armed with all the information, Keith went straight to Jerry, who after some initial scepticism soon realised the value of the material Keith had brought him.

"If this is genuine, then it is nothing short of scandalous. But how did you get hold of it? Nothing illegal, I hope."

"I'd rather not say."

"OK, then, let me put it another way. Did you ensure that when you acquired it, you left no trail behind you?"

"Yes," said Keith. "You could say it was found in the back of a taxi and no one would be able to prove otherwise."

"Good, that's exactly what I wanted to hear. We could break this in tomorrow's paper. It will be huge. However, perhaps we ought to contact Mr Colby for comment first."

"No, that is what we absolutely must not do. From what I've been told, this man has friends in very high places. If he wants to get this article stopped, he'll find a way of doing it. And that won't reflect well on you or me. But he can't stop it if he doesn't know about it, can he?"

"How come you know so much about this guy? I'd never heard of him until last week. I know I sent you down to the dungeon to check him out, but that was only for a couple of hours."

"It's called being an investigative journalist, Jerry," replied Keith sarcastically. "You know, what you employ me for? And I've done a pretty good job of it on this one, don't you think? As in, deserves a promotion level of efficiency?"

"One good scoop does not a career make," replied Jerry. "And you've not been here a year yet. However, I must concede that I like what I've seen so far. Keep it up, and we'll see what doors might open over the next few months."

"Right you are, Jerry," replied Keith, not unduly concerned at his lack of commitment. He knew he was a good journalist and had a good career ahead of him. He had already lived it. But getting involved in cases like the Colby one could only help accelerate his rise and it was all in a good cause. The bracelet seemed to think so too as it had been purring away in green mode throughout the whole operation.

When the story did break, he was pleased to see that Jerry had given him full credit for the story, which was all over the media by lunchtime, making the TV news with Kenneth Kendall. The story had well and truly made his name in the business but he couldn't help feeling a little apprehensive. In his visions, he had seen how ruthless James Colby had become in the alternative future and feared there might be some sort of retribution.

But thankfully, it never came. The backlash against Colby was so comprehensive that he had no way of covering his tracks. The day after the story broke, he faced the wrath of Chelsea fans, who scuppered any possibility of the takeover by staging a massive protest outside the ground. Not long after that he was arrested, with the police gaining a search warrant that gave them access to all the material in the safe, revealing all manner of other wrongdoings. Within a few days, his reputation was ruined and prison seemed a likely outcome. He wasn't going to be screwing anybody else over for a long time.

"I still don't understand how you found all this out, Keith," moaned Jimmy a few evenings later, as they sat watching England's first game against Belgium in the European Championships.

"Quite simple, really. While you were sitting in your room all last week studying your back copies of *Mayfair*, I was out doing some proper work."

"Yes, but you didn't tell me where you were going. I could have come with you. I thought we were a team."

"Sorry, old pal, but this was a hi-tech, very covert operation. No offence, but it may have proved a little challenging for a man who struggles to open a packet of Toffos," he said, referring to the tube of sweets that Jimmy was making heavy weather of unwrapping.

"Damn things, why do they make it so hard?" he said, wrestling with the dark blue wrapper in his desperation to get to the assorted flavours within.

"It's you, you're so bloody clumsy. You were as bad with that Rubik's Cube, talk about fat fingers."

"Finished it, though, didn't I?"

"No, you bloody didn't. You peeled off the stickers and stuck them back on one night when I was out. They're all loose now."

"No, I didn't. If I'm so ham-fisted, how did I manage to get them off?"

"I don't know, maybe you steamed them off with the kettle or something," replied Keith, as Jimmy succeeded in extracting a Toffo from the packet. They were individually wrapped in different colours, and the first one was red. Now, he faced his next challenge, getting the wrapper off the toffee. Keith watched with amusement, as Jimmy's woes continued.

"For goodness' sake, you really are hopeless. I don't know why you decided to become a photographer. I'm surprised you can even press the buttons on the camera. God knows what you must be like with a woman, blundering around down there."

"I doubt I'll ever get a chance to find out. Since Bob got out of hospital he won't let me anywhere near the Page 3 girls. I swear you put that Rachel off."

"I told you to choose Emma, but no, you went for Laura."

"She was pretty."

"Yes, but she couldn't smile. You heard what Bob said. That's every bit as important as the breasts. You only chose her to spite me because I suggested the other one, didn't you?"

"So what if I did? I don't have to do what you tell me all the time."

"No, you don't. It's a free country. If you choose to disregard my wise advice, then you have only yourself to blame for the inevitable bad outcomes. Now stop moaning and give me one of those Toffos."

"What flavour do you want?"

"Banana," replied Keith.

"But that's my favourite!"

"And I'm your favourite person. So what's the problem?"

"That's debatable, given your recent track record," said Jimmy, unwrapping the whole packet and tipping the contents onto the coffee table.

"There's only one banana one," said Jimmy.

"Bad luck, then," said Keith, leaning forward and grabbing it quickly before Jimmy could react.

"No, Keith," said Jimmy, trying to grab it back off him. He was determined not to let his flatmate get the better of him yet again. As they struggled for supremacy of the sweet they ended up wrestling each other to the floor, crashing into the coffee table as they went.

"Stop it, Jimmy," yelled Keith, dropping the toffee as they rolled around on the floor. Then they heard cheering and the shout of "goal" from the television. They stopped what they were doing and looked up.

"Yes!" exclaimed Jimmy. "England have scored! Who got the goal?"

"I don't know," said Keith, watching the replay on the ancient set. It was light years away from the Ultra 4K widescreen experience he was used to. "Wilkins, maybe?"

While he was looking, Jimmy looked for the Toffo on the floor but it had been ground flat into the manky carpet, right where there was a stain from where he had thrown up one night after a dodgy late-night doner from a shop called Kebabylon.

"Do you fancy a beer?" said Keith, getting up and heading for the fridge.

"If we've got any," said Jimmy. "It wasn't much fun being stuck here last weekend while you were supposedly banging some woman you met in a shop. While you were out on your big story. I was so bored waiting for you to come back that I drank it all."

"Bloody hell, you have," replied Keith. "Well, sod this, I'm going to watch the rest of the match in the pub."

Although he wasn't massively interested in club football, Keith did like to watch the big England games when they were playing in a major tournament.

"Why would you want to watch football in a pub?" asked Jimmy. "And how would you do it anyway? Most pubs don't have tellies."

"That's a fair point," said Keith, remembering that other than the FA Cup Final there were no live domestic games at all on TV in 1980. And even that kicked off at 3pm when all the pubs were shut. The first time he remembered watching a game in a pub was during the 1986 World Cup. Then, the landlord of his local brought his black and white portable downstairs and plonked it on the bar for everyone to huddle around. It was only when England and the other home nations were playing that you got to see live football on TV, and there hadn't been much for England fans to cheer in the previous decade. The team had failed to qualify for both the 1974 and 1978 World Cups.

"You'd be better off going to the off-licence at half-time and getting more beer in," suggested Jimmy, just as Belgium equalised. "Bloody hell, look at that."

"It will all be different in the future," said Keith. "The game's changing. Live TV games every weekend, pubs open all afternoon with big screens on every wall. Mark my words, it will be big business."

"Another prediction? You like bandying them around, don't you? Do you know what they're calling you in the office these days? The oracle."

"Not a bad nickname. Better than yours, which is the orifice."

"What? No, it isn't. You just made that up."

"Yes, I did," admitted Keith. "But it's good, don't you think? Perhaps we should try it out at work, see if it sticks."

"Please don't."

"Why not? It's better than the fat twat."

"No one calls me that, either. Now are you going to get this beer or not?"

"Why don't we just go out instead?" suggested Keith, who was bored with sitting in the flat. "Who cares about this bloody football anyway? I don't. We're not going to win so what's the point?"

"No, because when we go to the pub it's always the same. You start chatting up some bird and leave me on my own. Then you bring her back here and I have to listen to you shagging all night. These walls are paper thin, you know."

"Perhaps if you made some effort you could find a woman of your own. But the problem with you is that you spend so much time looking at pictures of naked women you've forgotten how to talk to a real one. They are actual people, you know. Try treating them as human beings rather than toys with two tits and a fanny put on Earth merely for you to play with."

"Bloody hell, what are you, some sort of feminist?"

"No, just stating a few facts. You go on like you are and you're going to stay a virgin forever."

"I am not a virgin!" protested Jimmy.

"Well, I've seen no evidence to the contrary. Now look, are we going to the pub or not?"

153

"Not," said Jimmy.

"Fine," said Keith with a sigh. He couldn't help feeling that he was wasting far too many nights just sitting around the flat. He was almost halfway through the year already and the thought that in another six months he would be back in his worn-out middle-aged body didn't bear thinking about. Then he had an idea.

"You know what we need?" he said.

"No, but I'm sure you're going to tell me."

"A holiday. The summer so far this year has been crap. Why don't we go down to the travel agents on Monday and book something?"

"Yes, a holiday, now that's a great idea!" exclaimed Jimmy, sitting up excitedly from his slouched position, suddenly full of enthusiasm. "Somewhere hot, where all the women go topless!"

"You're so predictable, Jimmy," replied Keith, but he was pleased that he was up for it. A chance to experience a holiday 1980s style could be a lot of fun. And the bracelet didn't disapprove. When Keith got back from the off-licence with a fresh supply of beer, they spent the rest of the evening discussing excitedly where they would like to go.

Unfortunately, the holiday would have to be put on hold for a while. That night, Keith had his most shocking dream yet, far surpassing anything that had come before. London was facing an unprecedented threat and it seemed that only he could prevent it.

July 1980

"Why are you only telling me this now?" asked Ted, his face contorted in a mix of disbelief and fear at the apocalyptic tale Keith had just told him.

"Because I didn't have all the details clear in my head until now," was Keith's reply, as they once again huddled and spoke in hushed tones in their little corner of the crowded newsroom.

It was the first Wednesday of July, which was men's quarter-finals day at Wimbledon. It was a tournament that Keith had been having nightmares about for several weeks, ever since the night he and Jimmy had fought childishly over the banana Toffo. Since then, England had crashed out of the European Championship in the group stages, further extending their failure to win a major trophy since 1966. When he did eventually get back to 2020, Keith, along with the rest of the nation, would be still waiting.

Now, Britain's attention had switched to Wimbledon and all the talk this year was whether Bjorn Borg, the incredibly popular Swedish star, could win a fifth successive title. Lurking on the other side of the draw was the brash young American, John McEnroe, who was already making a name for himself as a fiery character on the court thanks to his altercations with the officials.

Fiery was an apt description of what Keith had seen in his dream. It had all been rather vague, to begin with. He had envisaged Borg and McEnroe playing an epic final, one that would go down in history as one of the greatest of all time. He knew that to be true because he had already seen it but the scenes playing out in his mind were not the colour television of the BBC. They were grainy and washed out as if he was watching something filmed on an old black and white cine camera in the early twentieth century.

Everything was as it should have been up until a certain point late in the match when history deviated off course in the most shocking way imaginable. In the middle of a crucial fourth-set tie-break, Centre Court and the entire Wimbledon complex became consumed by an enormous fireball. At this point, his dream switched to a view of London from afar, where the unmistakable shape of a mushroom cloud was forming over SW19. There was no disputing what had occurred. It could only have been a nuclear explosion.

But how? And why? After the horrors of Hiroshima in 1945, no populated area had suffered a nuclear attack since World War II. When taking into consideration the sheer scale of terrorist activity in the decades since, it seemed remarkable that no group had ever managed to get its hands on the material to carry out such an atrocity. So, how had such a catastrophe unfolded here? With no additional information to go on other than what he had seen in the dream, it was hard for Keith to imagine a scenario where this could happen. This was long before the days of Al Qaeda, and despite the frequent bombings carried out by the IRA during this era, it was difficult to envisage them doing anything on this scale.

What other possibilities were there? It was still the height of the Cold War and relations were exceptionally strained at present, culminating in the USA's decision to boycott the forthcoming Summer Olympics in Moscow. But that was hardly a reason to nuke London. If it was down to a missile strike from the USSR it was hard to see what he would be able to do to stop it. And if it was, why? At one point he began to wonder if he was somehow to blame. Had all the ripples of the changes he had made since he had arrived spread out as far as the Eastern Bloc, giving Brezhnev cause to hit the big red button? It seemed unlikely because if someone sent back in time could cause something like that to happen, then surely whoever had created this bracelet to be passed on from person to person would have thought twice about it.

But they had, and whether he desired it or not, he was this year's custodian of the timeline and it seemed the responsibility fell to him. He had been disappointed all year that the jobs that he had been given had amounted to small beer. Now here he was, facing just about the biggest possible task that could have been thrown his way, preventing a nuclear detonation in London. And there was no doubt that it was real. Every time he woke up from the dream he was greeted with an angry red pulsing from the jewel on his wrist, warning him that this was very real, and happening very soon.

In the end, it turned out to be nothing to do with the Russians. Relations with Iran had been strained during the past couple of years with the American hostage situation and the embassy storming in London. It took a while for the full story to emerge, but slowly his dreams acquired more clarity, part of which was the revelation that there was a previously undetected Iranian terrorist cell active in the heart of London.

By the beginning of July, he had a pretty clear idea of how events were going to unfold. The explosion had not come from the launch of a missile but from a nuclear bomb, detonated on the ground outside the All England Club. The device was concealed in the back of a large blue transit van. In theory, this made it a lot easier to stop than something airborne, but it was still a daunting task. He had been good at science at school but defusing nuclear bombs had not been part of the syllabus. That was when he chose to approach Ted. If anyone would know what to do, it would be him.

"When exactly is this supposed to happen?" Ted asked, voice laden with trepidation. He knew from the experience of recent months that when Keith predicted something was going to happen it needed to be taken very seriously.

"The day of the final," replied Keith in a grave tone. "It's going to be between Borg and McEnroe, this Sunday. They are both playing their quarter-finals today."

Ted's mind raced, trying to process the enormity of the situation. Even he, with all his wartime experience, had never been confronted with anything on this scale.

"So we've got four days to stop it. Quite how, I'm not sure. I haven't got a Locksmith Larry on hand for this one. And we can't just ring up the authorities and tell them you dreamt it. You'll be dismissed as a crank at best, or at worst detained by the authorities."

"You believe me, though?"

"Of course I do. Your track record on this sort of thing has been impeccable. I have 100% faith in you, lad."

"But you don't know how to stop it?" said Keith with concern. There must be a way. He wouldn't have been given the task if there wasn't.

"Not right away. It's a pretty big thing to drop on someone, you know, far bigger than when you told me about the cancer. That was just about me but we could be talking about millions of deaths if we don't stop this, not to mention all the long-term consequences. You know, I don't feel comfortable talking about this in the newsroom. Give me some time to mull it over and then we'll go to the pub this evening and discuss it."

That evening, they went to the same backstreet boozer that Keith had taken Rachel to a few months before. It was busy, smoky, and noisy, but that was fine. There was no one there that they knew and those that were there were so preoccupied with their own conversations, they could talk freely and formulate a plan without nosey eavesdroppers.

"You said these terrorists were Iranian," stated Ted. "How did you figure that out?"

"I saw the van in vivid detail for the first time, last night," said Keith. "It looks nondescript from the outside, just pale blue, like a builder might use. But inside they've got an Iranian flag and a poster of the Ayatollah. Three of them drove the van there, and then they parked it and left. It was there for a good hour before the bomb went off."

"To give them time to get away, presumably. That's good. It means they're not suicide bombers and they don't want to die. That could be helpful."

"They could be apprehended?"

"Exactly," he said. "But also risky. If they are planning to detonate it by remote control, they could still hit the button if they get caught. Even if they don't want to die, they might resort to it under those circumstances."

"Maybe snipers could take them out instantly," suggested Keith. "Before they could detonate it."

"They could," said Ted. "But with the best will in the world, how are we going to persuade the authorities to do that, given the current political situation? Please, MI5, can you murder three Iranian nationals in broad daylight in cold blood just because we have a hunch they might have planted a nuclear bomb? No way is anyone going to green-light that."

"You know, I'm not sure it was detonated remotely. In my dream, I'm sure I saw a countdown clock on it. You know, like the ones in the movies where James Bond or someone comes along and defuses them with one second to go?"

"I'd like to hope we can cut it a little less fine than that," said Ted. "What I'm intrigued about is how they got hold of the material to make such a weapon in the first place. I mean you can't just go down to Do It All and ask them for a few ounces of plutonium. And even if you could get hold of it, storing and handling it is no picnic, believe me."

"There's no way to find out?"

"If any had gone missing from a nuclear power station or an RAF base I'm sure the authorities would know about it. But we would have been kept in the dark. They wouldn't want to worry the public. The good news is that I do still have contacts in the intelligence world. I could make some discreet inquiries."

"And about this cell? Could you find out about them too? It strikes me that it would be a lot easier if we could catch these guys before the day. I mean, we don't want to have to leave it until the nick of time."

"Possibly. But as you've said, you've no idea where this bomb is now. That van could be in some lock-up garage anywhere in London. We might be able to track down the terrorists, but it's the van that's the key element. If we catch them without the bomb, then who is to say it might not be rigged to go off at the set time anyway? It doesn't matter whether it is in Wimbledon or elsewhere, there is still going to be death and destruction on a wide scale. We can search beforehand but London is a big place and like I said before, it's going to be difficult to get assistance to do that without evidence. Which we don't have."

"What do you suggest we do then?" asked Keith apprehensively. He couldn't help fearing that this was going to go horribly wrong and he was going to end up dead. The fact that the bracelet remained permanently stuck on red wasn't reassuring either. Was he going to be the first custodian of the timeline to fail in the most spectacularly devastating way possible?

"I'll see what I can find out tonight," replied Ted. "Then we need to come up with a story we can convince the authorities with. We'll talk again tomorrow."

161

They parted company, leaving Keith to go home where he found his flatmate with his feet up on the coffee table devouring a large portion of fish and chips as he watched Hilda giving Stan Ogden a telling-off on *Coronation Street*. He didn't hang around for long, not being in the mood for the usual banter with Jimmy. It didn't seem right with what was currently hanging over his head.

After spending most of the evening in his room thinking things over, he had his most detailed dream yet. He could now see the precise working of the bomb which did indeed have a digital clock on it, counting down in big red LED numbers. He had joked about James Bond earlier but this truly was like a scene from the movies. Unfortunately, on this occasion there was no dashing hero coming to defuse it, thus, just as on every other night since the dream had started, Wimbledon and the surrounding area were vaporised.

Ted had plenty to tell him the next day when they took a tea break in the canteen.

"So it seems some nuclear material went missing from a power plant behind the Iron Curtain several months ago. How they got it out undetected is beyond me but I imagine some sort of corruption was involved, and that the material found its way onto the black market."

"However do you find this stuff out?" asked Keith.

"Oh, it's not for public consumption, believe me. Why do you think no incident like this has ever been reported in the press?"

162

"The obvious answer is because it's never happened before. But I guess you're going to tell me differently."

"You would not believe how close we've come to something like this occurring more than once before, in several places around the world. Very few people are in the know. The only reason I do is because of my past work with the intelligence services. These things come with a total news blackout. Technically, I'm breaking the Official Secrets Act just talking to you about this, but under the circumstances…"

He broke off as an enormously rotund tea lady came over, dressed in a floral blue dress with a plain navy apron tied around her waist. This was Beryl. When she wasn't out with her trolley doing her rounds, she was serving up meals and snacks in the canteen.

"Ooh, Ted, how are you? It's good to see you looking so well. Do you know, young Keith, he had a terrible cough a while back? Kept telling him to go the doctor, I did, but he wouldn't listen."

"I did in the end, Beryl," he remarked to the gossipy yet reassuringly warm and friendly woman. "And I'm all good now. Now what can we do for you?"

"Well, I saw you two over here with your cups of tea and I thought that's not enough to sustain two hardworking men, is it? So how about I bring you over a couple of my lovely jam and cream doughnuts? Fresh this morning I'll have you know, and only 10p each. Gorgeous they are, and I should know because I've had two myself. Well, I know you shouldn't but you've got to have some pleasures in life, haven't you?"

They agreed, if only to get rid of her. Everyone loved Beryl. She had worked at the paper for what seemed like forever and could rabbit on all day without you ever getting fed up with her, but today they had more important matters at hand. Keith couldn't help thinking as she came back with their cakes how much he missed people like Beryl. Where were the Beryls of the twenty-first century? They seemed to have gone extinct and been replaced by young baristas in coffee shops. Perfectly pleasant people, well, some of them anyway, but he'd take Beryl over them any day.

Alone again, Ted continued telling Keith about the consignment of nuclear material.

"It's certainly not beyond the bounds of possibility that it found its way here, but the logistics of transporting it are highly challenging. Smuggled in would be my guess, to some remote coastal area. I wouldn't have fancied being on the boat it came in on. As you can imagine, this stuff needs incredibly careful handling. Those involved may have been unwittingly exposing themselves to an unhealthy dose of radiation."

"And then what, they built the bomb here? I'm not being funny, but it's not exactly the sort of thing you can buy a manual for."

"Oh, they'll have had help. And lots of funding. Maybe even the Soviets are in on it. Who knows. But that's not important now. It's already built. Our priority is to stop it going off."

"I'm hoping at this point you're going to tell me you've come up with a plan," said Keith, biting into his finger-shaped doughnut causing a dollop of cream to drop out the other end onto his tie. "Bugger," he said, hurriedly trying to rub it off with a napkin.

"I have. Tell me what you think of this. I claim that I've been contacted by a member of the cell who is not as fanatical as the others. He's having second thoughts about murdering millions of people and wants out but he can't say anything to his cellmates because if he does, they'll kill him and carry out the plan anyway. By letting us know, he's asking for asylum and British citizenship, in return for information to stop the plot."

"Sounds plausible," said Keith.

"I let the counter-intelligence agencies know, who will know from my record to take the situation seriously. Then, on the day of the attack, they mobilise their forces to take down the terrorists, gain access to the van, and prevent the bomb going off."

"What if they can't? I mean, shouldn't they also evacuate London, just in case?"

"If they do that, then they will alert the terrorists that they are onto them. Then they will just lay low, still in possession of the bomb, and try again on a future date. No, we need to stop them now, it could be our only chance."

"Yes, that makes sense," said Keith, who saw to his relief that the bracelet had just started glowing green for the first time in days. It approved of Ted's plan then. He hoped it was right because this was an awful lot of lives to be gambling with.

Despite Ted's constant reassurances that everything would work out, and the comfort of the bracelet staying green on the morning of the final, Keith was consumed by fear. He had gone out with Jimmy the previous evening to a party in Covent Garden but hadn't been able to enjoy himself and had left early, claiming he wasn't feeling well. He had barely slept that night, tossing, turning, and sweating as he agonised about things going wrong.

In the morning, he was seriously tempted to get on a train and get out of London for the day. The bracelet didn't approve but what did it matter? He was no longer personally involved; it was all in the hands of the intelligence agencies. Perhaps it was his cowardice it was chastising, and it was right. What would fans of the Diamond Geezer think if they knew he was the sort of man who ran away? He needed to stay and brave it out. And anyway, surely he couldn't possibly perish in a nuclear holocaust here today. He was the custodian of a bracelet that had been passed down for generations to stop this sort of thing. It was hardly likely to lead him into a situation where it could potentially be destroyed.

Despite working all this out logically, there were parts of his body that didn't agree, and that led to him spending a good portion of the morning on the toilet. This didn't go unnoticed by Jimmy, who ribbed him mercilessly about it with a succession of very poor lavatorial puns. So preoccupied was Keith with the situation that for once he very much came off worse in the daily banter, and when Jimmy flicked on the television stating he wanted to watch the Wimbledon final, he found that he couldn't look away. He watched, entranced, feeling like a moth drawn to a flame, and as the match progressed inevitably towards that fourth set tie-break he steeled himself for the worst.

The relief as the tie-break concluded without incident and Borg marched on to his fifth title was like nothing he had ever felt. Later that evening, he met Ted who filled him in on the details. The intelligence services knew their stuff and had dealt with the situation swiftly and efficiently. The Iranians were apprehended shortly after parking the blue van close to the Wimbledon perimeter before the match had even started. It was quickly established that they had no way of detonating the device remotely, and operatives gained access to the van a good three hours before the bomb was due to go off.

The security forces determined, with the use of Geiger counters, that the makers of the device had at least gone to the trouble of making it safe to handle. No radioactive material was leaking into the general environment, which made it a lot easier to keep secret from the public what was going on. A team kitted out in hazmat suits might have attracted rather a lot of attention outside Wimbledon on their most important date of the year.

The device had been professionally made but was relatively simple for the highly trained bomb squad to defuse. It was all rendered harmless with hours to spare, without any movie-style last-minute suspense. The public never had an inkling of what was going on and that was the way it stayed. As Ted had previously explained, there was always a news blackout on anything of this ilk. The last thing the security forces wanted was to put ideas in the heads of every terrorist organisation in the world that this was the sort of thing they should potentially attempt. Therefore, the world would never know of Keith and Ted's heroic intervention.

It was another job done, and for the first time, Keith recognised just how important the bracelet was. What he had just done, aside from saving millions of lives, had avoided an event that would have had timeline-shattering implications. Everything else he had done over the year had been trivial by comparison. If this was the one big event he had been sent here for, and everything else in the year was just minor tinkering, then that would suit him just fine. He had no desire to go through another day like today.

It was all very well saving the world, but perhaps it was time he thought about his own needs. He hadn't done a lot in terms of making his life better while he had been here, having baulked at the initial suggestion of using the experience to become a better person. That sounded all goody-goody, and not like him at all. But then, if he did take a long look in the mirror he couldn't deny that he didn't like some of what he saw. Maybe he ought to at least think about using some of his remaining time here in the past to make changes that might positively impact his future.

But in the meantime, there was a holiday to be had. With the Wimbledon disaster averted, he had certainly earned a break. A week after Borg had claimed his fifth consecutive title, he and Jimmy headed to their nearest branch of Lunn Poly to book their getaway.

August 1980

"I told you we should have gone to Majorca," complained Jimmy for about the eighth time, as he lay beside Keith on the sun-drenched poolside terrace in front of their modest pension apartment. They had spent the morning recovering from the previous evening's hangovers on the white plastic sunbeds but it was now starting to get too hot.

"As I have said, several times, Majorca was all booked up for August," said Keith, pulling out his sun cream and rubbing a little onto his nose, which he was worried might be starting to peel. He got to his feet and manipulated a nearby parasol into a position where it would give him some respite but even in the shade he was still too hot. He looked at the small pool in front of them glistening in the brilliant Aegean sunshine and thought about taking a dip. It would get him away from Jimmy's endless moaning for a few minutes. Personally, he couldn't see what the problem was. He was more than happy with the sleepy seaside village which was a few miles away from Crete's more lively holiday destinations.

"But there's nobody here!" complained Jimmy. "We've been here five days and haven't had a sniff of a chance at pulling. There hasn't even been anything to pull. It's all old people. You should have checked where we were going when you booked."

"As I have also explained more times than I care to recall, the accommodation was allocated on arrival. All we knew is we were coming to Crete but we didn't know

169

where. That's why it was so cheap. I mean, what were you expecting for £79 each? Raffles? And it's not that bad anyway. Yes, the room is a little basic, but look around you. It's beautiful here and we've got this place all to ourselves. Why this obsession over trying to pull women all the time?"

They were the only ones on the poolside terrace which also overlooked the shore below. The view was magnificent. The midday sun hung high in the clear blue sky, casting a brilliant shimmer upon the tranquil waters of the Mediterranean. The sea stretched out as far as the eye could see, its surface rippling with a gentle breeze that brought a slight relief from the heat of the August sun. The water's hues shifted from deep azure near the horizon to a lighter, inviting turquoise closer to the shore.

The small pension apartment where Keith and Jimmy were staying opened out almost directly onto the swimming pool. They were virtually sunbathing on their front porch. The building was painted in the traditional white colour of nearly all the buildings in the village, with dark blue shutters and doors giving off a rustic old-world charm that Keith found incredibly calming. It was about as close to paradise as you could get, at least in Europe.

Between their apartment and the sea were many olive trees, their gnarled trunks and branches dotting the landscape. It was the archetypal view of Greece as displayed on a million picture postcards. As Keith lay back under the shade of the parasol, he could still feel the heat of the baking sun slipping through small gaps in the weathered straw material. When Jimmy wasn't spoiling the mood with his complaints, the only sounds he could hear were the gentle lapping of waves against the shore and the chirping of insects from the olive groves.

He loved it. But Jimmy didn't. The difference was that despite being in his young body and having taken full advantage of that back home, he had no desire to go on some wild holiday with a load of other young people. He was, after all, still over sixty mentally. It had been a busy year, considering all the interventions he had been required to make in the timeline, and all he wanted to do right now was relax and recharge his batteries for whatever was still to come. But Jimmy was still in his early twenties and it wasn't what he had come on holiday for at all.

"It's alright for you," said Jimmy, resuming his diatribe. "You get women all the time. It's harder for me. That's why I wanted to go on a proper holiday, like one of those Club 18-30 ones. They reckon it's almost impossible not to get laid on one of them."

"I'm sure you'd manage not to," said Keith. "Now come on, just take a proper look around you. You are in one of the most beautiful places in Europe and you're having an authentic experience. You want to savour this while you still can before mass tourism rides roughshod over almost every available corner of Greece and Spain."

"I don't want an authentic experience. Speaking of which, I don't like the food, either. What was that horrible pink stuff you made us order in that restaurant last night?"

"Taramasalata," replied Keith. "It's considered a delicacy."

"It was like fishy Angel Delight," said Jimmy. "Disgusting. And it wasn't even a proper restaurant, just a couple of tables in some family's back garden."

"But that's the whole point," said Keith despairingly, feeling beads of sweat beginning to form on his forehead. He wasn't sure if it was just the sun that was getting him overheated or his frustration with Jimmy's ignorance. "That's what gives this place its rustic charm."

"Well, I heard they've got proper fish and chip shops in Majorca. And all the women are gagging for it."

"Fine, we'll go there next year, then," said Keith, knowing he would be long gone by then. "But can we at least try and make the most of this while we are here?"

"Suppose so," replied his sullen companion, picking up the five-day-old copy of one of the tabloids they had brought with them from the aeroplane the previous Saturday. "I wonder what's happening back home?"

"Who cares?" said Keith, and he meant it. One of the things he found refreshing about this holiday was that they were completely cut off from their life at home. They had no mobile phones to be pestered on by Jerry or anyone else from the office. Contacting England, should they have some pressing need to do so, would be a challenge and there were no English newspapers in the village. There were no televisions in the tavernas and no other evidence that a world outside this small community existed at all. A major disaster could have occurred somewhere in the world and they would have been completely unaware of it. They were totally cut off and it was absolute bliss.

The bracelet had lain dormant the whole time they had been away. He had wondered when they had booked their trip if he was being guided towards Crete to sort out a timeline issue here but it seemed that wasn't the case. It was giving him a break. He had grown much more comfortable with the device now that he knew where he stood with it. If he thought about making a bad change to the timeline, it would let him know. If he did a good deed he got the green seal of approval. He had resented this in the early days but wasn't bothered anymore. On minor issues it wasn't compulsory to follow its advice, and he had gone against it on the odd occasion, such as when he had taken up smoking again. Apart from that one time it had scalded his arm in the betting shop, it hadn't punished him for minor transgressions.

What he found odd was the selective nature of the bracelet's opinions. It might offer a judgement on whether he smoked or not, but remained silent about other matters with far greater societal consequences. Something that had been bugging him ever since he arrived was the constant presence of Jimmy Savile everywhere he went. He was on posters, on the radio, on the television and in the papers, via which he constantly publicised his charity work. He couldn't even get away from him in Greece where he could see a picture in the newspaper that Jimmy was reading of Savile laden with bling running a marathon. The bracelet seemingly had nothing to say on the matter so it was time to take matters into his own hands. When he got back to London he was going to try to expose him.

"You know the other problem with this place?" said Jimmy. "There's no bar."

"We don't need a bar! We're literally five yards from the fridge in the apartment. There's plenty of bottles of Amstel in there."

"Yes, but I don't want beer. I want something exotic, to make me feel like I'm on holiday. Like a Piña Colada or something. You know, like in that song."

"That song alone is enough to make me never want one. Now listen, I want to ask you about something. What do you think of Jimmy Savile?"

"I think he's very good on *Jim'll Fix It*. Though he's a bit old for *Top of the Pops*."

"Yes, right, but what about as a person? Don't you think he's a bit creepy?"

"Maybe a bit but that's all part of his act, isn't it? You know what these celebrities are like. They all have their little quirks to make them stand out. Like Larry Grayson on *The Generation Game*."

"This bloke's got more than a few quirks," replied Keith, before going on to lay out the truth about Savile in stark detail.

"I'm sorry, Keith, this is nonsense. If he's spending a lot of time at the hospital, it's only because he wants to help sick children."

"He's the sick one!" exclaimed Keith. "And the truth needs to come out now, not after he's dead."

"You know, I'm starting to worry about you, Keith. All this stuff you keep coming out with. It all sounds a bit delusional to me. Last week you were going on about Rolf Harris which was even more ridiculous. How could such a gentle man even dream of doing the things you said? Now. I get it, you don't like Jimmy Savile but there's no need to make up all this stuff about him. I know you want to be a top tabloid journalist and all that but this is going way too far."

"Oh, whatever, Jimmy. I can't be bothered to argue, it's too nice a day. But when we get back to London, I'm going to make Jerry listen."

"Good luck with that," replied his friend, getting up from the sunbed and diving, or to put it more accurately, belly-flopping into the pool.

Keith looked at his blubbery and sunburnt friend, wallowing about in the water. He had overdone it on the first day and had been peeling ever since. Keith rarely suffered from that problem, having more olive skin, which he also protected liberally with sun cream. Other than his nose, the rest of his body seemed to cope with the sun rather well. He looked down at the bracelet, and a thought suddenly struck him.

"Jimmy," he said, a couple of minutes later when his friend hauled himself out of the pool. "Have I got a white line on my arm here? As if I had been wearing a watch in the sun?"

"No, nothing," replied his friend, reaching for a towel.

That was odd. It was as if it wasn't there at all. Yet he hadn't been able to put sun cream there either so in theory it ought to have burnt. Never mind, this was one mystery he couldn't be bothered to worry about. As Jimmy sat back down, he got up and jumped in the pool himself. After a brisk ten lengths up and down, he suggested they get out of the midday sun and down to the village to find a taverna.

Two days later they were on a plane heading for home. Back in the newsroom the following evening, Keith tried broaching the subject of Savile with Jerry but got nowhere.

"I think all that sun's gone to your head, my lad! Got any proof?"

"Well, no, but if you were to put a surveillance team on Stoke Mandeville hospital when he goes there on one of his overnight visits, you wouldn't come back empty-handed."

"Sorry, Keith, you're not on. Jimmy Savile is one of the most well-respected and loved entertainers in this country. What sort of paper would we be if we tried to destroy him?"

"I don't think I want to answer that," said Keith, recalling some of the character assassinations carried out in the past on people who had been deemed ready for the chop.

"Good, then I suggest you go and get yourself reacquainted with your desk, while I think of something more appropriate for you to be working on."

Back in his usual corner, Ted, who had overheard the conversation, offered his advice.

"You're wasting your time there, son. Savile's untouchable."

"You believe me, then?"

"Of course. When do I ever not? You're not the first to try and go down this road when it comes to Savile. It's been tried before."

"Why didn't Jerry say anything, then?"

"Because it's more than his job's worth. A couple of years ago, we had a woman come in here with all we needed to expose him. She had dates, times, witness reports, the lot, not just about herself, but others too. And Jerry was all up for it, to begin with."

"What happened?"

"Let's just say that Jimmy has got friends in high places. Very high places. And the message came down in no uncertain terms to drop it. This woman was similarly rebuffed by the police. And the BBC."

"But that's outrageous."

"Oh, I quite agree. But I'm afraid that is the way the world works."

Keith contemplated things for a few moments. So the establishment couldn't help him. What if he took Savile out himself? Even, dare he say it, kill him? Could he do that? Would he be justified in doing that?

Not according to the bracelet, which began pulsing red at his thoughts. He just couldn't understand why, but then, that night, he had his answer.

In his dreams, he envisaged several scenarios where he carried out the grisly deed of doing away with Savile. While all his plans looked good on paper, they all ended the same way. He achieved his aim and despatched Savile, no problem. But no matter how much he tried to cover his tracks he always got caught and ended up being sentenced to life in prison, reviled by everyone in Britain as the man who murdered a national treasure. The message could not be clearer – 'do this and it won't end well for you'.

It seemed he had no choice but to drop it. Then, the very next day, a similar but far more pressing scenario presented itself. What's more, this was a case in which he was sure he could make a more meaningful impact whilst staying within the law.

When he got into the office, one story alone was dominating proceedings. He knew something big was going on the moment he walked through the doors. The room was different on days like this. It was packed and the activity was feverish, with people dashing around, and all the phones ringing off the hook. A hive of activity on this scale only happened when there was a major story. And as far as 1980 went, this one was about as big as it got.

"What's going on?" he asked Gordon, the first person he could get the attention of.

"It's the Ripper! He's struck again!"

Of course, thought Keith, *the Ripper*. Not Jack the Ripper, though he recalled the nickname Wearside Jack being incorrectly attributed to this killer by the police at one point. This was the Yorkshire Ripper who had claimed a string of victims in the late 1970s and early 1980s. Oddly, although Keith had been back in this newspaper office for nearly eight months, this was the first time he could recall any mention of him. Why was that? It had been one of the biggest news stories of the era.

"When?" was all he could think of to ask.

"Last night. And we all thought he had stopped. It's been nearly a year since the last one."

That might explain why the story had passed him by. There hadn't been any murders in 1980 until now. But now, the case was well and truly back in the spotlight.

"You'd better speak to Jerry," said Gordon. "It's all hands to the pump today. We're going all out on this one. A five-page special. I heard him telling Bob earlier that we're going to have to put tomorrow's tits on page seven."

"Oh, I'll be speaking to Jerry, alright," said Keith. He had refused to listen regarding Savile but this time he was determined to make him cooperate.

"You're late, Diamond," barked Jerry, who was looking even more stressed than usual. It was a hot day outside and even hotter inside, causing his Bobby Charlton cut to stick to his head with sweat, forming small drops of moisture which rolled down his forehead. It wasn't a good look.

"By like, two minutes," said Keith, looking at his watch. He didn't mind the heat, having been acclimatised by his recent trip to Crete, but he could see most of the others suffering. He expected the ever-increasing number of mainframe terminals were contributing to their discomfort. They gave out an enormous amount of heat.

"Yes, well, I need you on this right away. I want you to find out as much as possible about the latest victim. Ted will give you the details."

"Hang on a minute, Jerry. There's something I need to tell you."

"There always is with you. It's going to have to wait," said Jerry, waving him away, leaving Keith to make his way over to his desk where Ted had some details released by the police about the latest victim in the Ripper's gruesome spree.

"Marguerite Walls, forty-seven, from Leeds. A civil servant. Not the usual type he goes for. That's if it even was him. I mean, since the police started closing in, he's gone quiet."

"Have they, though? Started closing in?"

"You heard the tape," said Ted, referring to a recorded message from a man with a Sunderland accent that had been the focus of the police's investigation for the past couple of years.

"Yes, and it was a fake," said Keith. "That's why he hasn't been caught. The police are barking up the wrong tree."

"Let me guess, you know all about it," said Ted. "I would expect nothing less. I believed you about Savile but as you discovered, he's untouchable. If you do know something about this case, perhaps this time you can make a difference."

"I do know all about it. I know who he is and I know he's known to the police. The only reason they haven't got him yet is because they've thrown all their eggs into the wrong basket which means that the real culprit doesn't fit their profile. His name is Peter Sutcliffe and he is from Bradford, not Sunderland."

"Then you've got to let the police know," said Ted. "If you can lead them to him, then he won't be able to kill again."

"Believe me, if I can, I will," said Keith, noting the bracelet growing green again. At least it seemed to approve this time. "But what can I do?"

"Contact Yorkshire Police. Express your concerns. But you'll have to give them something solid. You do know that people contact the police all the time with spurious information, don't you? It's why they created an offence of wasting police time. Otherwise, every Tom, Dick and Harry with a grudge would be trying to drop their enemies in it every five minutes. Or you'd have weird fantasists like Mad Harry leading them a merry dance."

"I can only tell them what I can remember," said Keith. "Which probably isn't a lot that they don't already know. All I do know is that he is going to be caught very soon. I'm sure his last victim was killed in 1980."

"Get onto them, then. Ring them, write to them, do whatever you can."

"Do you think Jerry will help? I mean, deploy me to work on the case? If I've got a lead?"

"You can try," said Ted. "But I wouldn't hold out too much hope."

Ted was right. Jerry didn't want to know and what's more, after he tried, he earned himself the dreaded call into the meeting room for a dressing-down.

"Now look here, Diamond, you're a bright lad, but if you want a career in this game, you've got to play by the rules. You've got a degree in journalism, so you should know how this works."

"I thought it was a prerequisite of our job to find stuff out. You know, like the police do. Or don't, in this case."

"Yes, and what's the one thing the police need before they can arrest someone? The same thing we need before we hold the front page. Evidence. Cast-iron evidence. And what do you bring me? Claims that one of Britain's most loved entertainers is a paedophile and the supposed identity of the Yorkshire Ripper. For which, I should add, you do not have a scrap of evidence. Where would we be if we started printing this stuff willy-nilly? There's libel for a start, and that's not the half of it. You start bandying around names of Ripper suspects and you could prejudice any case the police might be building. You're out of order, and it needs to stop."

"If you let me investigate these things properly I could uncover the evidence. But every time I ask, you shoot me down."

"Because I don't know where you think you're getting your information from but it all sounds like an overactive imagination to me."

"Ted said that everyone knows about Savile. But you've all been silenced."

"With the greatest respect to Ted, he needs to learn to keep his mouth shut. As do you. Now I'm officially warning you, Keith, I don't want any more of this. Otherwise, I'm going to have to think seriously about your position here. Do I make myself clear?"

"Crystal," said Keith, disappointed by his boss's attitude, even though it was totally predictable. It was also extremely frustrating. Here he was, sitting on information about two of the most evil men in modern British history, and he seemed unable to do anything with it. How many more would suffer at their hands due to his impotence?

Disobeying Jerry's instructions he did telephone Yorkshire Police to voice his suspicions about Sutcliffe but it proved to be a difficult conversation. They assured him his information would be taken on board, but were generally dismissive about it, even going so far as to suggest that being a London-based journalist he couldn't possibly have a clue about what went on up north. After he hung up he felt demoralised and that they had not taken him seriously at all. As a final throw of the dice, he wrote an anonymous letter detailing everything he could remember about Sutcliffe in the hope someone might take notice of it, even if it had come from a London postmark.

After a few days during which the latest murder dominated the headlines, other stories inevitably came along to take over. In this case, no news was not good news. Every day, as August gave way to September, he hoped that the story of Sutcliffe's arrest would break but nothing was forthcoming. There was no sign that he had made any sort of difference at all.

September 1980

"Soho?" asked Jimmy, his eyes sparkling with anticipation. "Hell, yeah, I'm definitely up for a night out there!"

"I thought you might be," replied Keith, with a knowing smile. Soho held a notorious reputation in the 1980s as a place with a vibrant but seedy underbelly that enticed many seeking a good time. It was home to strip clubs, sex shops, and a notorious red-light district – all elements that had surely piqued Jimmy's interest. "I know why you want to go, but we're not going for that."

"Ah, come on, Keith, we can't go for a night out in Soho without seeing some strippers."

"Why do you need to see strippers? You've got a room plastered with pictures of naked women."

"Yes, but they're just pictures, aren't they? I mean, this is an opportunity to see real women. Naked – in the actual flesh!"

"I guess that would be a novelty for you. Alright, if we get our business concluded in time, perhaps we could go and check out one of these sordid establishments. But bring plenty of money. Those places aren't cheap."

"And what is our business, exactly?" asked Jimmy, curious about Keith's motivation for their latest excursion. "Is it work-related? Should I bring my camera? I could get some tasty pictures in Soho. Both for the paper and my private collection."

"We're going to a pub in Soho. A lot of famous people hang out there. Maybe we can get an interview with one of them. So yes, you can bring your camera."

The bit about interviewing celebrities was a lie but Keith couldn't tell him the real reason they were going. He was just glad the bracelet was giving him something useful to do as he had been feeling increasingly disillusioned as September had worn on. The frustration he felt at his inability to do anything about Savile and Sutcliffe had continued to grow, and as weeks passed with still no news of any arrest, he had to conclude that his attempts to reach out to Yorkshire Police had failed.

To take his mind off it he now had something else to get involved in. Interestingly, this meant going back to the very place where he had first taken possession of the bracelet. Once again, he had been led there by a dream. In this one, he had returned to the pub in Soho where he had gone after he had been sacked from ChatFM. In his dream, the pub ended up being reduced to a smoking shell by a devastating fire. This was something he was sure had not happened in the original timeline so his task was clear – to prevent the blaze.

The pub in question had a reputation of being a haunt for some of London's most celebrated boozers, none more so than the legendary Jeffrey Bernard, a racing journalist and gambler who had led such a colourful life that he even later had a West End play written about him. Keith had seen Jeff and his entourage of fellow drinkers many times in the flesh over the years and had even bought him a drink once. It hadn't led to much of a conversation, though, as it was a Saturday lunchtime and Jeff was engrossed in the racing pages.

By the time Keith and Jimmy were on their way to Soho on a warm early autumn evening, Keith knew exactly what he needed to do having foreseen what would happen in precise detail. He knew what was going to cause the fire and when it was going to happen. All he needed to do was prevent it, though that might not be as easy as it sounded in principle.

Night had long since fallen by the time they found themselves walking through the seediest part of Soho, the darkness merely adding to the sleazy atmosphere. Forty years from now this area had been cleaned up but in 1980 it was still a den of iniquity. Bright flashing neon signs surrounded them, advertising strip clubs, peep shows, adult cinemas and more. It all had a mesmerising effect on Jimmy, whose curiosity got the better of him as he stopped outside one of the shady cinemas.

"Do you fancy going in here?" he asked.

"Not particularly," replied Keith. "Are you really that desperate?"

"What's wrong with going to see an adult film?"

"Well, that depends on your viewpoint. If your idea of entertainment is sitting in a darkened room wanking with a load of other men, then fill your boots. But forgive me if I don't join you."

"Oh," said Jimmy. "I didn't realise it was that bad."

"Of course it is! I mean, why do you think they're all wearing those long macs in this weather?" said Keith, watching as two furtive fellows went in, nervously looking around to check no one they knew had seen them. "It's to hide what they're doing."

"How about one of these strip clubs, then?"

186

"Maybe later," said Keith. "I want to get to the pub before last orders. We're supposed to be finding someone famous to interview, remember? We can come back here afterwards. Some of these places open way into the small hours."

In truth, Keith had no intention of venturing into any of the many dubious establishments. He had only dangled the idea like a carrot to get Jimmy to come along. He knew that he might need his friend's help later, but for now would prefer it if he remained oblivious to the real agenda.

It was gone ten by the time they arrived at their destination, and as Keith had envisaged it was not too busy. It was Tuesday night, and he was delighted to see that Bernard was indeed perched in his usual spot, holding court in front of half a dozen others including a couple of very famous faces.

"Isn't that...?" began Jimmy.

"It is indeed," replied Keith, recognising the unmistakeably curly hair of the actor who played Doctor Who. "And one of the other chaps with them is the artist, Francis Bacon."

"Do you think they'll talk to us, or let us take any pictures?" said Jimmy, pulling out his camera just as the middle-aged barman came over to serve them.

"You can put that away for a start," said the man rather abruptly, looking them up and down. "The regulars don't like to be photographed. Are you two journalists?"

"How did you know?" asked Jimmy.

"I can spot you a mile off. That suit, for a start. It's too small for you."

Jimmy was still wearing the same faded cream suit that he had been wearing since they had been at university.

"It wasn't when he bought it," said Keith. "He's grown out of it."

"It's bloody awful. And yours isn't much better," he added, which annoyed Keith, as he thought he looked rather snappy in the navy suit that he had recently purchased from Moss Bros. Perhaps he should have just come out in his usual leather jacket and jeans. It wasn't as if they were actually working tonight, after all. He had just donned the suit to dupe Jimmy into thinking this was a real assignment.

There was an awkward pause as the man looked them up and down, seemingly weighing up if they were worthy to drink in his establishment. Then finally, he asked what they were having.

"Two pints of lager, please," replied Keith.

"Lager. You do surprise me," said the man, beginning to pour. "Now you two just behave yourself and don't bother my other customers. I don't trust journalists."

Keith knew from the man's demeanour that he should have kept his mouth shut but could not resist blurting out, "Isn't that Jeffrey Bernard from *The Spectator* over there? He's a journalist."

"He's a regular. I look after my regulars."

"I expect they look after you, don't they? He's probably paid for this place three times over."

"That's enough of your lip, lad. How old are you? Twelve? Jeff's forgotten more about journalism than you'll ever know."

Keith held his tongue, not wanting to risk getting thrown out, as he pondered how he was going to broach the subject he had come to talk about. The initial exchanges across the bar hadn't filled him with confidence. He looked over the man's shoulder to a fridge behind the bar which contained various ales and soft drinks. This was the focus of what he wanted to talk about, and he could already see that the lights on the fridge were flickering slightly.

"You know, you ought to get that fridge looked at," said Keith. "It sounds like it's on the blink. It could be a fire risk."

The barman shot him a glare. "Do I come down to your newspaper office and tell you what stories to put in tomorrow's paper? No. So don't tell me how to run my business."

There was a roar of laughter from the end of the bar where one of the regulars had just come to the end of a lengthy anecdote, leading to a cry of "drinks all round". As the barman moved away to attend to them, Keith and Jimmy took the opportunity to grab a table at the other end of the bar.

"What was all that about?" asked Jimmy. "Why did you start going on about the fridge? I'm surprised he didn't chuck us out."

Keith paused, considering his reply. He knew exactly what was going to happen. The fridge was faulty and was going to catch fire and set the whole place ablaze in the small hours. Somehow he had to prevent that from happening, and it did not look as if he was going to get any cooperation from behind the bar. How was he going to explain this to Jimmy?

"That fridge is dodgy. It's a fire hazard. It could burn the place down if it's not dealt with."

"What makes you such an expert?"

"Umm, it's my brother," said Keith, saying the first thing that came into his head. "He's a fire safety officer."

"You haven't got a brother."

"Cousin, then. Does it matter? The point is, if we don't get rid of that fridge, this place is toast."

"Come off it, Keith, how can you possibly know that?"

"I'm telling you, if we don't get that fridge out of here, this place will be a smoking cinder by morning."

He knew this was a flimsy argument but in his dream, he had seen himself and Jimmy trying together to haul it out of the pub. It was a heavy piece of kit and a two-man job.

"You know, I wonder about you at times," said Jimmy. "You come out with the most random crazy stuff and just expect me to go along with it."

"I'm never wrong, though, am I?"

"That's the most infuriating thing about it. Come on then, clever clogs, how are we going to get it out of the pub? Waltz behind the bar and start wheeling it out? Without being noticed?"

"No, of course not. We need to wait until the pub has closed and everyone has gone."

"By which time, we'll be outside."

"Not necessarily. We could hide."

"Where?"

"In the toilets."

"He'll check them at closing time."

"He won't check the ladies," said Keith, looking around. There were only about twelve people in the pub, all of them male. "We'll wait until the last minute, then sneak in."

Jimmy was extremely sceptical but Keith was confident they could do it. He had already pictured them succeeding in his dream. They just had to wait for the right moment, right after last orders had been called when the barman was in demand from the regulars, desperate to get another round in before kicking out time.

"What are they doing?" said Jimmy, watching fascinated as the group appeared to be playing some sort of game that involved putting their fists out and then opening them.

"They're playing spoof," said Keith. "It's a game where you have to guess the total number of coins in everybody's hand. The loser buys the drinks. Now get ready, this is our moment."

He knew it was time because the bracelet was telling him, and exactly as envisaged, the barman reached up and rang a large brass bell hanging above the bar. Timing it to perfection, they scampered into the ladies while the regulars were engrossed in their game.

"It doesn't feel right being in here," said Jimmy. "And I need the toilet."

"Well, you're in the right place."

"Not in here. It doesn't feel right using the ladies."

"You'll just have to wait then. We won't be in here long."

As it turned out, they were. Although the pub was soon officially closed, the regulars were having a lock-in. Judging by the regular cheers, more games of spoof and more rounds were in progress. It was a good couple of hours before things went quiet, and Jimmy was not happy.

"I can't believe you talked me into this," he said. "We could have been in a nice strip club now."

"There's no such thing as a nice strip club," said Keith. "They're all horrible."

"That's not what you said last year when we went on that stag trip to Amsterdam."

"Yes, well things have changed a lot since then."

"Haven't they just. You know something, Keith? I think you're starting to get old before your time."

If only he knew, thought Keith, who was distracted and hadn't noticed that the bracelet had been giving him the green light to go back out into the pub. Now, it began flashing red again, with regular, fast pulses, like it had in the past when things had been urgent.

"Come on, we've got to go," he said, as they exited the ladies into the now darkened pub. The curtains were

192

shut tight, with not an inch of gap anywhere. Presumably, this was done so as not to draw the attention of the police during the earlier lock-in. The only light was coming from behind the bar where the malfunctioning fridge was making a fizzing and crackling sound.

"Jimmy, get the doors unbolted," said Keith. "But quietly. We don't want to wake the landlord."

"I need a piss first," replied his friend, hopping from one foot to the other, desperately trying to hold it in.

"Bloody hell. I told you to go in the ladies."

While Jimmy was in the gents, Keith went behind the bar and began seeing if he could ease the fridge out on his own but he quickly realised they had left it too late. As soon as he touched it, it burst into flames, just as Jimmy came back in.

"Shit!" said Keith, stepping back hurriedly just in time to avoid a set of singed eyebrows. "Find a fire extinguisher, quick."

Thankfully the pub's fire equipment was up to scratch and they were able to put the blaze out quickly. But it wasn't fast enough to stop the fire alarm going off. In a panic, they raced for the door, sliding across three heavy bolts to get it open before the landlord came down. Thankfully for them, once it was unbolted they didn't need an additional key and they were out into the cool night air just before they were spotted. They ran off down the street and around the next corner, after which they could finally relax.

"Do you think anyone saw us?" said Jimmy, aware that there had still been quite a few people milling around in the street when they had made good their escape.

"What if they did? We haven't stolen anything. And when the fire brigade comes they'll see someone put the fire out. They'll identify the fridge as the source and condemn it, so we've done the landlord a favour. No one's going to come looking for us unless they want to give us a reward."

"OK, good. So can we go to a strip club now?"

"If you want to waste your money in one of those places, go ahead. But I'm getting a taxi home. Coming?"

Reluctantly, Jimmy followed him towards a row of black cabs, and they headed back to the flat.

On reflection, it hadn't been a bad night's work. He hadn't stuck exactly to the script because they hadn't ended up removing the fridge from the pub as he had originally planned. Arguably, this was a better outcome, as they couldn't be accused of theft. Happy that the pub would still be standing in the future just as he remembered it, he was able to go to sleep pleased at another job well done.

In the cold light of the following morning, he didn't feel so content. The chilly start to the day was a reminder that the year was growing older. Once again the feeling began to nag at him that despite the good deeds, he wasn't making the best use of the opportunity he had been given. As he moved into the final quarter of the year, he resolved to himself that he must not waste it.

October 1980

"Keith, I'm sorry to say that you've drawn the short straw, mate," said Jerry, grinning with the look of a man who was not sorry at all as he towered over Keith's desk, his dank, loose hair flopping down in front of his eyes.

"Eh? What do you mean?" asked Keith, who was getting fed up with Jerry dumping all the crap jobs on him. "I haven't got to do the racing again, have I?"

"Nothing so mundane," said Jerry, pushing his hair back onto the top of his head to cover his bald spot. "You'll like this. I've got a couple of work experience girls coming in. One's going in with the typesetters and the other's coming in here. She's got some crazy notion she's going to be a journalist or something. A week in here should knock that out of her. Anyway, I want you to babysit her."

Keith perked up at this news. This could be the moment he had been waiting for all year. It was highly probable it was going to be Nathalie, who was someone he had thought about a great deal. He was no longer angry about her throwing him out of ChatFM. In hindsight, he had probably had it coming, and the way he had conducted himself in his meeting with her had hardly been his finest hour. When he thought back about the cheap jibes he had made about Barbie dolls, amongst other things, he winced. Now perhaps was his chance to do something about it.

"What do you want me to do?" he asked.

"Oh, not much. Ted is away in Spain for a week's holiday, therefore I thought she could sit at his desk. Just tell her a bit about what we do here, then give her some photocopying or filing to do. And once Beryl's finished her rounds, get her to make the tea. It'll be good practice for when she gets married."

"I'm not being funny but what's the point of her coming in here for the week to find out about journalism if all we're going to do is get her to make tea?"

"Look, Diamond, I don't want her here any more than you do."

"I never said I didn't want her here, did I?"

"Well, I wouldn't, if I were in your shoes. An annoying teenage girl to look after for the week, going on about pop stars and makeup and other girlie shit. The only reason she's here at all is that I'm giving the deputy head from her school one. I said I would do this as a favour. And, as I said, Ted's away, there's a free desk, and you're the youngest one here – so the obvious choice. Good luck. She's in reception when you're ready. Her name's Natasha or something like that."

"Nathalie?"

"Yes, that's it, Nathalie. Good. Well, you toddle off and get her and don't do anything I wouldn't do," said Jerry, flashing him a conspiratorial look that Keith didn't care for. It was obvious what the old perv meant.

Although he was looking forward to seeing Nathalie, Keith knew the next hour or two was going to be tricky because he knew the baptism of fire Nathalie would receive when she walked into the newsroom. Although he remembered little about it from before, he suspected to his shame he had joined in with it. She had told him as much on the day of the sacking but he was still

196

adamant she was wrong to identify him as the culprit in the bum-slapping incident.

He felt a strong sense of trepidation as he made his way to reception, but with a hint of anticipation too. He had been through all sorts of experiences over the past nine months, many where lives had been at risk, including his own. Yet somehow, the encounter he was about to have trumped all that had come before. For the first time, this was an opportunity to do something to alter the course of his life for the better, both now and in the future.

What would she be like? He thought about the smart, confident businesswoman he had come up against before. She had been the finished article and had wiped the floor with him. What would this version, less than a third of the age of that older incarnation, be like?

His first thought as he spotted her standing in the reception area was an obvious one and that was how young she looked. This was exacerbated by her choice, or possibly the school's, to come to the office in school uniform. It was fairly standard for the era, consisting of a knee-length plaid skirt, a crisp white blouse, and a dark blue cardigan. Her socks came up almost to her knees, not leaving a lot of flesh on display, which was fortunate, considering the lion's den she was about to enter. He was more worried about her ample chest which was bound to draw comments, despite her tender age. Those he worked with didn't care one jot about that.

He wouldn't have recognised her from her face alone, so innocent and youthful but what gave her away was her hair. It was just as it had been before, a lush head of brown, shoulder-length curls, which she kept off her face with a single, thin headband.

Her demeanour in the reception area was a far cry from the assured poise of the older woman he had met at ChatFM. Her nervousness could be seen, in the first instance, in that she hadn't taken a seat. She was standing, looking at some of the old front pages on the wall, shifting her weight from one foot to the other, almost as if she needed the toilet. Just before she caught sight of him he saw her nibble slightly at her lower lip, another subtle sign of apprehension.

It was hardly surprising looking at the content of some of the front pages proudly displayed on the wall featuring headlines relating to various sex scandals. This was no place to be sending a young girl. Keith had to question what the deputy head could possibly have been thinking, even if she was supposedly calling in a favour from Jerry.

"Nathalie?" he asked tentatively, the tone of his voice betraying that perhaps he was even more nervous than she was.

"Yes," she replied, turning to look at him with her hazel eyes, and a face full of nervous excitement. It was clear she had come here with great expectations, and he felt awful remembering how swiftly those dreams had been shattered by her experiences here. He simply could not allow that to happen again.

"I'm Keith," he said, "Keith Diamond," and he held out his hand to shake, rather than attempting to kiss her on the hand or cheek, which no doubt some of his colleagues might attempt later. He also didn't give her any of his Diamond Geezer shtick. He'd gone right off that lately.

"I'm one of the journalists here," he explained. "I started last year. Now, before we go into the newsroom, let's go and have a chat over there."

He gestured towards the large leather sofa opposite the reception desk where most visitors waited. He had rehearsed in his head what he was going to say but he was still worried he was going to mess it up.

"Listen, Nathalie, I thought we ought to have a talk before we go in. You see, this place probably isn't going to be like anywhere you've ever been before."

"Oh, I realise it's probably going to be hard work," she said. "I'm not under any illusions. My careers officer explained how pressured the newsroom environment can be."

"It's not the work you've got to worry about. It's the people. Let's just say, women's rights aren't something that have made much of an impact around here yet."

"You mean it's a very male-dominated environment."

"That would be putting it mildly. And with men who retain old-fashioned values, to put it politely. Look at it this way. We're a paper that glorifies in publishing tawdry stories about the sex lives of the rich and famous, as well as splashing pictures of women's breasts all over Page 3 every morning. To many of the men that work here women are nothing more than sex objects, and they talk about them accordingly."

"It can't be as bad as all that, can it? I mean, a lot of the boys at my school are like that. I'm sure I've heard it

199

all before. Don't feel you need to protect me. I'm not a little girl."

"Yes, but that's the point, at your school they are just immature boys. Here you are going to be dealing with dirty old men leering over you and making lewd comments. And believe me, that's what you're going to get when you go in there."

"But presumably you're not like that? You wouldn't be saying all this if you were. You'd be joining in with the rest of them."

"No, I'm not," said Keith, feeling like a bit of a fraud, because he knew that was exactly what he had been before. "That's why I'm warning you now so it doesn't come as such a shock when you get in there. The other thing is that none of them will give a rat's arse for your interest in the profession. To them you will be eye candy, someone to make them tea, and someone to dump any crappy boring task onto that they cannot be bothered to do themselves. And I don't think that's fair. You've come here to learn about journalism so I will try and teach you as much as I can. But I'm not the boss so I can't promise anything."

"It sounds horrible," she said pensively, clearly wondering what she was letting herself in for. "But I'm so glad you warned me."

"Just try and rise above it," said Keith. "Because things are not going to be like this much longer. The world is changing, and a time will come when women are given the respect they deserve, not only in the workplace but in all walks of life. It's up to the likes of us to bring about that change. So whatever they say, you just let it run off you like water off a duck's back."

"I will," she said determinedly. "Thank you, Keith."

"Let's do it, then," he replied. "Expect the worst."

When they entered the newsroom, the reaction surpassed even his expectations. As they walked through the room, there were the inevitable wolf whistles, followed by a comment of "nonce" from Gordon as they passed his desk, a predictable slur given him being in the company of a schoolgirl.

"Let us know if you need any extra tuition, sweetheart!" called out Bob, from the other side of the room where he and Jimmy were sifting through some topless photographs. Bob, who had not been in the best of health of late, had finally relented and allowed Jimmy to get involved with the glamour photography and he had been making the most of the opportunity.

There was also a shout of "cracking pair" from the far side of the newsroom, but he didn't manage to identify who that had come from.

When they made it to Keith's corner, he turned to look at Nathalie to see how she was coping and was pleased to see that she seemed remarkably calm.

"Everything OK?" he asked. "I mean, I did warn you."

"I'm so glad you did," she replied. "Yes, this is quite the place, isn't it," she said, casting her eye about through the clouds of smoke at the busy newsroom, phones ringing, green screens glowing, and the tapping of fingers on the keyboards. More of the computer terminals were being installed all the time and he now had one of his own.

"I'm afraid you'll have to use a typewriter," he said, gesturing at one of the few remaining models on Ted's desk that the older man still clung fiercely to. "But I'll show you how we access the mainframe from my desk. Have you used a computer before?"

"No, we don't have any in school," she said. "They've been talking about getting some, though."

"These things are the future," he replied. "Before long there will be one on every desk and in every home in the country. You see that typewriter on Ted's desk? In less than a decade the only place that will be fit for will be a museum."

"Wow," she said. "The future's going to be amazing, isn't it?"

Keith thought about the present day and the day of forty years in the future. Yes, some things were better, but others were a lot worse. He had no desire to shatter her illusions though, so he just went along with it.

"I'm sure it will be. Technology is advancing at such a rate, isn't it?"

At this point, they were interrupted by Jimmy who had come along to try to ingratiate himself with the office's new young temporary recruit.

"Alright, Keith," he began. "Are you going to introduce me to your new friend?"

"This is Nathalie. She's here for her work experience," replied Keith, flashing him a look to indicate he was not to say anything inappropriate. But his warning was lost, as Jimmy's eyes were fixated on the girl. Predictably, it was one specific part of her body

202

he had been drawn to, the one that had led him to want a career in photography in the first place.

"Yeah, well the thing is, Bob over there, he's the chief photographer, asked me to ask you how old you are?"

"I'm fifteen," she said.

"Oh, pity," said Jimmy. "When are you sixteen?"

"In January. Why do you ask?"

"Jimmy!" said Keith firmly, in a second attempt to warn him but he was again ignored. Well, sod it, then. If Jimmy was going to make himself look like an ignorant arse, let him. Then when he'd gone too far, Keith could ride to the rescue.

"Ah, I'm a January baby too," said Jimmy. "The thing is, me and Bob were wondering if, when you're old enough, you'd be interested in a bit of topless modelling work? Maybe with a sexy schoolgirl angle, you know the sort of thing."

Yes, that was far enough, thought Keith, who said, "Jimmy!" firmly for a third time, finally provoking a response.

"What?"

"Fuck off."

Jimmy looked first at Keith, then at Nathalie, who were both looking at him disapprovingly.

"Right you are," said Jimmy, quickly realising that the game was up, and he scuttled away with his tail between his legs.

"I did warn you," said Keith, turning back to her.

"You did. Thanks for telling him to f…I mean go away."

"There'll be plenty more where that came from. Think you can handle it?"

"Bring it on," she said, smiling, much to Keith's relief and a growing confidence that everything was going to work out OK. For the rest of the afternoon, they were largely left alone until Nathalie left at 4pm. Once she was out of the way, Jerry came over and from the confrontational look on his face as he approached, Keith could see a difficult conversation might be looming.

"Right, what's your game?" he demanded.

"What do you mean?"

"I mean, I told you she was here to do odd jobs and make the tea. Yet, you've kept her at your desk all afternoon. Want to know what I think?"

"Go on," replied Keith, already suspecting the predictable conclusion that Jerry would have drawn.

"I think you're planning on giving her one, aren't you?"

"For fuck's sake, Jerry, she's fifteen."

"You know what they say, if they're old enough to bleed."

"That's an absolutely vile remark and you know it."

"Yeah, well, nothing the others aren't saying. You're the talk of the office. How old are you? Twenty-two? A good-looking young journalist taking advantage of the situation, that's what they reckon."

"I'm sorry, but that's bollocks. She's here to learn. She's interested in journalism. What's the point of having her here if we don't teach her?"

"This is an adult environment. It's not *Play School*. People like her don't belong here."

"But you're the one who brought her here in the first place! What sort of impression of this place do you want her to take back to the school? This teacher you're knocking off, nice, is she?"

"Tidy bit of stuff. And she's only thirty-six. I'm thinking of leaving the missus for her once the kids are old enough."

"You don't want to do anything to sully your new bit of stuff's opinion of you then, do you? I'm doing you a favour. I've shown her how we retrieve information from the mainframe, how we submit reports, and explained all about the production cycle. This is all useful stuff and when she goes back to school, she'll tell them how much she's learned and your mistress will be grateful you gave her the chance."

"Maybe. But I still don't trust your motives. Do you remember what you said to me when I interviewed you for this job?"

"Not precisely. It was a long time ago."

"It wasn't that long ago. It was only last year. I asked you what your favourite hobby was and you said, 'chatting up birds'. And since then you've been knocking them off left, right, and centre. You've got a reputation. So what am I supposed to think?"

"I can assure you that I have no improper intentions towards her whatsoever. Unlike some of the scum in here. Bob's already sent Jimmy over here with some scheme to get her onto Page 3."

"That's as maybe, but I think it might be better if I split you two up. I've got a job for you tomorrow. I want you to go to the British Motor Show at the NEC. British Leyland is launching a new car, the Mini Metro. You must have heard about it. I want you to get a train up there and cover the launch. Take Jimmy with you."

Keith thought quickly, before making a suggestion.

"Look, Jerry, why don't you let me take Nathalie with us? We can be there and back on the train during the working day and it'll be a fantastic experience for her."

"You must be joking!" replied Jerry. "I can't let you two go off to Birmingham taking a fifteen-year-old with you."

"Just get permission from the teacher you're shagging," said Keith. "You don't want to rock the boat with her remember? And imagine the trouble you could be in if your wife was to find out," he added, lacing this line with just enough menace to let his boss know what he was implying.

"Are you blackmailing me?" asked Jerry incredulously. "You're getting way too big for your boots, lad. I've been wondering for a while now if you're really suited to working here. Perhaps it's time we reconsidered your position."

"If you reconsider my position, your wife will definitely find out," said Keith, fixing his eyes on Jerry's, determined not to blink first.

He couldn't believe how audacious he was being. If Jerry called his bluff he could be out on his ear but the jewel in the bracelet was glowing green with approval, so he was confident he was doing the right thing.

"Alright, Diamond, you win – for now," said Jerry, admitting defeat. "But I've got my eye on you."

A couple of phone calls later and their trip to the NEC was all planned. Thus, the following morning Jimmy, Keith, and Nathalie found themselves zooming up the Chiltern Line on an InterCity 125 towards Birmingham. Jimmy was noticeably subdued on the train. He had been read the riot act in no uncertain terms by Keith when he had got back to the flat the previous evening. He was under no illusions about what would happen if he tried any more conversations along the lines of the previous day.

As the three of them entered the bustling motor show, they were blown away by the sheer magnitude of the event. The main hall was packed with throngs of people swarming around, their excitement almost infectious. Families, car enthusiasts, and anyone who was anyone in the motor trade were there, and the various car manufacturers had spared no expense in showcasing their new creations. Honda, Mazda, Toyota, and others had created dazzling displays as they launched their new models at the biggest car show in the country.

And it wasn't just the cars that were attracting the crowd's attention. Many of the manufacturers had decided to draw attention to their vehicles by adorning them with glamorous women. Scantily clad, they posed like ornaments, leaning seductively against the polished chrome. Cameras clicked and flashed, capturing the provocative scenes, a tactic that was meant to add allure to the car launches. Jimmy was quick to join them, knowing this was exactly the sort of thing that Jerry would want to put in the paper.

Amid all the glitz and glamour, one car was the talk of the town – the Mini Metro. With the way the car industry had been going it was practically British Leyland's last great hope. The beleaguered car manufacturer had stumbled through recent years beset by strikes and launches of various cars of dubious reliability and longevity. It wasn't far off becoming a laughing stock, yet somehow there was huge excitement about this new family car which had neither glitz nor glamour.

Jimmy, full of enthusiasm, turned to Keith, his eyes sparkling with anticipation. "What do you reckon, Keith?" he asked, gesturing to the bright red model of the British car industry's latest dubious attempt to drag itself out of the doldrums. "Are you going to give it a good write-up?"

Keith's response was laden with the cynicism of someone who had seen it all before. "I don't see what's so special about it, quite honestly," he remarked. "It will probably be like every other car we make in this country – falling apart due to rust within ten years."

He spoke from experience, his memories filled with images of cars slowly crumbling on the streets of Britain. The domestic motor industry's reputation for producing reliable, long-lasting cars was in tatters. The Mini Metro would however become a success for a while. Lady Diana Spencer owning one in 1981 before her marriage to Prince Charles had given it a huge boost. Her endorsement had sent the cars flying off the showroom floors and they remained popular throughout the 1980s. But by the mid-2000s, they were almost all gone, rusted into oblivion.

"Well, I like it," said Nathalie. "I would certainly consider getting one."

"You aren't old enough to drive," said Jimmy.

"I will be in a couple of years. If I go to university outside of London, I'm going to need a car."

"Take my advice, don't get a Metro," said Keith. "You're far better off going for something like a Volkswagen Polo or a Nissan Micra when you do get on the road. And as someone who has always championed buying British, I say that reluctantly but it's true."

"I don't think I've heard of a Nissan Micra," said Jimmy.

"Still in development," said Keith hurriedly, realising he might have put his foot in it. It must be too early for the Micra.

After an exciting day enjoying the heady atmosphere of the show, the three of them made it back to London by teatime. Jerry was pleased, meaning that Keith's write-ups and Jimmy's photos featured heavily in the following day's edition.

Reunited with Nathalie in the office the next day, Keith continued to be subjected to jibes from the other journalists. He found it quite boring how they kept implying there was something untoward about his relationship with her, so he tried to look unperturbed. He was doing nothing wrong and as far as he was concerned it was all down to their dirty minds. It did make him question whether he wanted to carry on working at this paper in the long term. Should he seek employment somewhere a little more enlightened? Or stay here and try to change the culture from within? He consulted the bracelet, which seemed to indicate the latter option. Fair enough.

On Thursday afternoon, another opportunity for a jaunt out of the office presented itself.

"Just had a call from Ted," said a stressed-looking Jerry, who had come looking for Keith in the basement where he was showing Nathalie how the microfiche system worked. "He was due back today but is stuck at Alicante airport. Apparently, the air traffic controllers have gone on strike again."

"And you are telling me this why?" asked Keith, knowing he was about to get lumbered with another job. Every time anyone was sick, on holiday or absent, it was him that Jerry turned to. He wasn't sure if that was down to his journalistic skills or because he was still the youngest.

"He is supposed to be covering Maggie's speech at the Tory Party Conference in Brighton tomorrow," said Jerry. "You'll have to do it instead."

"Ooh, can I go?" asked Nathalie, her eyes lighting up with excitement. "That would be an amazing opportunity."

"I'm not sure about that," said Jerry. "I had to call in a couple of favours last time so you could go to the NEC. And what with all the rumours flying around the office about you two, I don't think it's a good idea."

"Forgive my frankness but that's bullshit," said Keith. "There's absolutely nothing going on."

"That's right, there isn't," said Nathalie, speaking up with the firm confident tone that was an indicator of the woman Keith would meet again, forty years in the future. "My parents and teachers would have no problem with me attending the conference. Ask them if you don't believe me. I'll be quite safe with Keith. And I assume Jimmy will be coming too?"

"He will," said Jerry, relenting grudgingly. "Alright, if your parents and teachers give written permission, you can go. But, Keith, you are responsible for her. If anything goes wrong, on your head be it."

"Right you are," said Keith, and with that settled, they spent the rest of the afternoon preparing for the conference.

On Friday they travelled down in a busy train carriage, which contained many other conference attendees, judging by the number of blue rosettes on show. As the train sped through the picturesque English countryside, the conversation was all about the day ahead, about which Nathalie remained very excited.

"You're full of enthusiasm this morning," remarked Keith. "I have to say, I didn't have you down as a Tory fangirl."

"Oh, I'm absolutely not," she said. "My family are Labour through and through, always have been. My dad's the union rep at the textile factory where he works. He can't stand Maggie."

"So why was he happy for you to come to this, then?"

"It's a chance to get inside the Tory mind-set, isn't it? See what makes them tick."

"Like going behind enemy lines?" replied Keith.

"Exactly," said Nathalie. "If I do go into journalism, I want to focus on politics and that means trying to see things from all the different points of view."

"Let's hope all the political journalists in the future feel the same way you do," said Keith, knowing depressingly that they would not. By the dawn of the 2020s, people were more tribal than they had ever been.

"Well, I love Maggie," said Jimmy. "I think she's what we need to get this country back on its feet."

"What do you think, Keith?" asked Nathalie, with a genuine look of curiosity in her eyes.

"Not a lot, to be honest," said Keith. "And that's not just me sitting on the fence. I don't feel an allegiance to any one party. I think they're all a bunch of crooks."

That was how he genuinely felt, which made it all the more remarkable the direction his career would later take. From around 2009 onwards, politics had been a key part of his show on ChatFM, during which time he had interviewed almost every major politician of the day, including three Prime Ministers. It hadn't been something he had intended, having started out doing a light-hearted topical afternoon show. But he could hardly turn down the flagship breakfast show when it was offered, could he?

The conference took place at a plush hotel on the seafront. The main lobby was a lively hub of chatter as men in well-tailored suits and women in elegant dresses mingled, exchanging political banter and opinions.

There might have been a recession looming but these people didn't seem short of money. It was an event that would be remembered as the one at which Margaret Thatcher gave her famous, "the lady's not for turning" speech. Nathalie watched the Prime Minister enraptured, despite her left-leaning tendencies, sensing that she was witnessing a truly historical moment. She still didn't like the Tories, though, and judging by some of the people she had seen around her at the conference she wasn't going to be changing that point of view any time soon.

On the train back to London, Jimmy predictably disappeared in search of the buffet car, leaving Nathalie and Keith sitting side by side engrossed in discussing the finer details of what had been said at the conference. It was the final day of her work experience, and obviously aware this might be her last chance she decided to turn the conversation to more personal matters. She turned to Keith, her eyes brimming with gratitude and admiration.

"Keith, I just wanted to say before we get back, how wonderful this week has been. I could never have imagined when I first arrived how much I'd get to see and do. It's been amazing!"

Keith smiled, his eyes full of warmth and a tinge of pride. "All part of the service," he said modestly. "And you weren't too horrified by the others in the newsroom?"

"Oh, them," she said dismissively. "Perhaps I would have been if you hadn't been there. But you're not like them. You're different."

She turned to look at him, eyes full of anticipation, and then to his surprise she leaned closer and attempted to kiss him. Keith was taken aback and quickly pulled away.

"Whoa, what are you doing?" he exclaimed.

"I'm sorry," she said, a flicker of hurt in her eyes. "You've been so nice to me. I thought you wanted to."

"That's what they all think in the office," said Keith, speaking gently, as he didn't want to upset her. "But I thought I'd done enough to prove that I'm not the same as them. My intentions have only ever been honourable."

"It's my fault, I misread the signs," she said, with just a hint of a tear forming in one of her eyes.

Keith reached out, placing a reassuring hand on her arm. "Look, Nathalie, I was put in a position of responsibility to look after you. What sort of bloke would I be if I took advantage of that? In the future, they'll have a word for that – it's called grooming. But that's not what I'm about. All I wanted to do was give you a decent grounding in the world of journalism. If it had been left to any of the others, they would have had you making tea all week at best, and leering at your tits and slapping you on the arse at worst."

"That's what makes you special," she said, as a genuine smile began to break through her initial disappointment.

"I'm not that special," said Keith, who knew that he wasn't. Perhaps he had paid too much attention to Nathalie to try to compensate for his past behaviour, leading her to jump to the wrong conclusions. And who had he been doing it all for, her or him? Was it just to save his own skin, to stop future Nathalie from sacking him? Perhaps a bit but he had genuinely enjoyed the company of this younger version and had wanted to help her. He hoped she would grow up to be a happier person than the revenge-driven woman he had encountered back at the start of all this.

"Well I think you are," she said. "Can I see you again?" she asked, her voice filled with a mix of hope and longing.

"Not for a while," said Keith. "You need to go back to school and work on getting the qualifications you need to go to university and train for a career in journalism – if that's what you still want to do."

"More than ever."

"Good," said Keith, nodding approvingly. "And then, when you're a fully-fledged journalist in the future, I am sure our paths will cross again."

"Thank you. You've been so good to me," she replied, just as Jimmy returned and sat down opposite them, placing a cup full of weak-looking tea and a cheese sandwich on the table in front of him.

"What have you two been talking about?" he said, taking a sip from the cup. "Bloody hell, this tea's cold. And as weak as piss."

"Oh, nothing important, right, Nathalie?" said Keith.

"Right," she said, smiling, as the train rolled on, wheels clacking rhythmically against the rails as it sped them home to London.

November 1980

"This is a bloody swizz!" complained Jimmy, as the closing credits rolled after the second episode of the new season of *Dallas*. "We still don't know who did it."

They were sitting on a plush leather sofa in their much-improved living accommodation. Finally, they had got away from the Whitechapel hovel and were now sharing a much nicer home.

"I already told you, it was his sister-in-law, Kristin," said Keith. "And we don't find out until the fourth episode."

"What's the point of that? Build it up to be this big mystery and then keep people hanging on for weeks?"

"You just answered your own question," replied Keith. "We want to sell a lot of papers, right? So if we get a huge story, we want to drag it out over a few days. Same with this. They're going to get four weeks of massive viewing figures and all the advertising revenue that goes with it."

"I still don't see why you're so sure it's Kristin."

"Inside information, mate," said Keith aloofly, in a way that he knew always infuriated Jimmy.

"Yeah, you get a lot of that, don't you?"

"Annoying, isn't it?" Keith was revelling in the fact that after almost a year Jimmy was still none the wiser about his knowledge of the future. He had thought about telling him early on but found this more entertaining. By keeping Jimmy in the dark he could constantly infuriate him with his clever-Dick predictions that inevitably came true. He knew it made him come across as an insufferable know-it-all but that was OK because he didn't do it to anyone else. Just Jimmy.

He looked around the spacious living room, relishing their new surroundings. It was a proper two-bedroom house in one of the nicer parts of Bethnal Green. It had come part-furnished, hence the posh sofa, enabling them to finally dispose of the hideous, garish old one. It even had a garden, or to describe it more accurately, a backyard. It was light years better than the old place but Keith knew he was not going to be there for long.

Of late, he had been giving his future much contemplation. After the big events of the summer, the bracelet had eased off. It seemed as if his biggest tasks were behind him, leading to a rather anti-climactic feeling. As autumn wore on, the weather got colder, and the leaves fell, there was a growing feeling of dread inside at the thought he was going to have to go back. He didn't want to, and who would?

The real kicker was when the clocks went back at the end of October. It was always one of the most depressing weekends of the year and he wondered why the world persisted with the archaic practice. It was just another reminder that the year was running out. He felt like someone who was enjoying a fortnight holiday somewhere hot and sunny, with just a couple of days left before having to fly back to reality. It wasn't quite over yet but the fat lady would soon be singing, and his looming departure weighed heavily on his mind.

To compensate, he threw himself ever more enthusiastically into the young, single lifestyle, going out nearly every night, having frequent casual sex, and soaking up every bit of culture that he could. This included several visits to the cinema in Leicester Square to see fondly remembered films such as *Private Benjamin* and *Airplane!* He had lost interest in the cinema in the future dismissing it as woke, formulaic crap, but back in 1980, it was so much better. His first trip gave him one of the most nostalgic moments of his whole year – watching the classic Pearl & Dean advertising trailer.

His greatest indulgence was music. In the future, he could listen to almost every song ever recorded via the streaming services but what he couldn't do was see the bands perform live in their heyday, which was now. The music scene in London was vibrant and almost every weekend some legendary band or other was performing, many before they had achieved success.

The bigger bands favoured venues such as the Hammersmith Odeon but he also had a soft spot for the lower-key places, such as the Hope and Anchor pub in Islington. He had spent the last two Friday nights there with Jimmy, seeing first The Specials and then Madness. It simply didn't get any better than that. Good as these nights were, they ultimately only depressed him afterwards, hammering home the mediocrity of the life in the future he was soon to return to. And speaking of his future, come mid-November he was faced with what could only be described as an impossible dilemma.

It happened when Jerry sent him across to the typesetting room on an errand. This was a department of mostly female employees who prepared the finished copy for publication in the newspaper. Just as with

Nathalie's recent arrival, Keith had been anticipating this encounter for some time too. He knew that someone was coming to work in this department sometime later in the year who was going to alter the course of his life. Or not, depending on what he decided to do. Despite knowing this day would come, it still came as a shock when he came face to face with her for the first time.

Penny. The woman on whom his life from this point onward pivoted. She wasn't the love of his life, far from it. There was just one thing that set her apart from the many other women he had been involved with. He had got her pregnant.

He walked into the room, document in hand, and there she was, enthusiastically looking up at him with the eagerness of someone on their first week in a new job. Returning her gaze, he was struck by her youthful beauty and look of innocence. Unlike most of the women in this office, she used just a minimum of makeup, preferring the natural look, and was able to carry it off, blessed as she was with a flawless complexion. With her bright green eyes radiating vitality, and her straight blonde hair cut in a bob, it wasn't hard to see why he had been attracted to her. This was a very different woman from the one he had later come to resent.

At twenty, she was just a couple of years younger than him. Unlike many events in the past, he still recalled this first meeting and chatting her up all those years ago. Establishing that she had just split up with her boyfriend, he had quickly asked her out, leading to a brief dalliance that went on for a few weeks. He had enjoyed her company at that time as she was into the same music as he was. He could remember Jimmy getting most disgruntled that he preferred to take her to gigs rather than him, particularly as it was obvious Jimmy was keen on her himself,

He wouldn't have gone so far as to say they were boyfriend and girlfriend, though he knew that she probably saw it that way. He had even tried to be honest with her, explaining he wasn't in it for the long haul but she had said she was fine with that. He got the distinct impression that she was playing the long game, hoping that he would get so used to her company that they would officially become an item eventually. It was a forlorn hope because that was something he had no intention of at that time – with her or anyone else. Until, a few weeks into 1981, she got pregnant.

It came as a complete shock because she had assured him she was on the pill, leaving him facing one of the most important decisions of his life. He hadn't been ready to give up his single lifestyle for any sort of commitment, let alone one that involved raising a child. He didn't really care much for her either, if he was being honest. Sure, she was great fun to go to gigs with, have a drink with, and go to bed with, but that's all it was. She was more like a mate, a female version of Jimmy perhaps, but certainly not someone he had any sort of romantic feelings towards. What was he going to do?

In the end, under pressure from all sides, he did what was commonly referred to as 'the decent thing' and decided to stand by her. That meant marriage, thus, against all expectations, he found himself walking up the aisle of a small church in Kensington one bright July morning in 1981. Then he walked back down with a heavily pregnant bride beside him.

His life changed completely. That morning, when he left the house in Bethnal Green with best man Jimmy beside him, was the last time the two of them would share a home together for many years. Fortunately, her parents were not short of money and were able to help them buy a new-build house in the north London suburbs but he wasn't content living there at all. Although he still got to go into the city for work every day, he missed living in the heart of London.

The first couple of months before baby Jacob arrived were OK but after that, things rapidly deteriorated. A life that had been all gigging, drinking, and shagging less than a year before had morphed into sitting in his dull new home at night watching *Blankety Blank* and *Play Your Cards Right* surrounded by the aroma of stinky nappies. It wasn't his idea of fun and he was pretty sure it wasn't hers, either.

The problem was simple and obvious and they were equally to blame. They should never have got married and they both knew it. He didn't love her and she didn't love him really, either. She thought she did at the start but what she loved was the idea of him – the dashing young journalist who had swept her off her feet and now they were going to live happily ever after. It was a fairy-tale. He wasn't that sort of man and had told her enough times but she had deluded herself otherwise until it was too late. It wouldn't be long until the wheels came off.

As he climbed the ranks of the journalistic world he got the opportunity to travel out of town frequently. Invariably he ended up sleeping with other women while away. He did try to keep things together with Penny but as time went on she became increasingly bitter towards him, and it was obvious the days of the marriage were numbered.

When it did all blow up in 1986, it turned out he wasn't the only one who had been having affairs when she got pregnant again. Bearing in mind the two of them hadn't had sex in several months, he knew the baby couldn't be his, and things soon took an unpleasant turn. In the end, she admitted that the father was Kevin Duckworth, a local plumber whom Keith had called out to fix a broken pipe while he was away in Mexico covering the World Cup. But there was no apology. As far as she was concerned, she was entitled to seek comfort elsewhere due to his neglect. Looking back at it now, he had to admit she had a fair point.

There was a bitter and protracted divorce case which he came out of very badly. She inevitably got the house as well as custody of Jacob, and spent the following years slowly poisoning her son's mind against his father. By now, Kevin had got his feet well under the table in his old home and gradually he took over the father role to Jacob. Keith barely saw his son for years, then on his eighteenth birthday Jacob declared that Kevin was now his real dad, and he wanted nothing more to do with his natural father. As a final insult, he changed his surname from Diamond to Duckworth.

Keith had agonised over the years about how much he was to blame for this turn of events. Yes, he had got Penny pregnant in the first place. Yes, he had cheated on her throughout their marriage. Yes, he had married her for the wrong reasons.

It was easy for him to take all the blame, but something Ted had said to him just before he retired, when the wedding plans were in full flow, had nagged at him all these years.

"She's played you good and proper, mate."

This had come after Keith had confided the doubts he'd been having at the time, in particular the accidental nature of the pregnancy. Ted's opinion was that she had likely never been on the pill and had been out to trap him.

"You wouldn't be the first bloke it's happened to and you won't be the last," he had added.

It had made him wonder. He had never seen her pills but had no reason to doubt her. Perhaps he should have taken more responsibility himself and worn something. Back then, before the AIDS scare blew up, if a woman said she was on the pill then her word was usually good enough. But there was no point crying over spilt milk at that point, he had responsibilities, so despite Ted's warnings the wedding went ahead.

This had been all water under the bridge until he had come back to 1980. But it wasn't now. As he looked at Penny, busy with her typesetting, he knew this was a chance to change things. He could simply avoid her this time. He could spare them both years of pain and misery, simply by ensuring that no relationship ever developed between them. And then, the whole course of both their lives would change dramatically and hopefully for the better.

It was a lot to ponder, and right now he was on the spot. He knew this was the day he had first chatted her up so he could start changing things right now. After a brief bit of eye contact when he first came in, he studiously avoided looking anywhere near her desk for

223

the remainder of his short time in the room. He just handed over the documents he had brought to one of the others and hot-footed it out of there in double quick time.

It was only when he was walking back to the newsroom that the implications of what he was doing struck him.

Yes, he might be sparing the two of them a lot of heartbreak but what about Jacob, his only child? If he didn't get together with Penny as had originally occurred, then his son would never be born. In short, he was condemning him to death. Some might even contend that it amounted to murder.

Was that a valid argument? At this point in time, the child had not yet been conceived. If the events leading up to that event never happened then he would simply cease to exist. There would be no pain and no heartbreak for anybody but Keith himself. Despite their estrangement, he had genuinely loved his son when he was little and had many fond memories of those first few years. He could have been a brilliant dad and would have been if he had just had children in better circumstances. But he never got the chance again.

Despite his playboy lifestyle, he had not ruled out the possibility after his divorce that one day he would find the perfect person, settle down, and live happily ever after. But his experience with Penny had left him with a fear of getting too close to anyone. There had been a few relationships in later years, and he even lived with people for the odd year or so, here and there, but if the spectre of commitment raised its ugly head, he tended to cut and run. In the end, the person he ended up living more years with than all those girlfriends put together was Jimmy.

But even Jimmy left him in the end. Despite being hopeless with women in his younger years, he finally found someone in the new century and tied the knot in 2011, by which time he was into his fifties. They still saw each other regularly and met up once a week to record their controversial podcast, but as far as living arrangements were concerned, after Jimmy got married Keith was on his own for good. Or so it seemed.

What difference would it make if he never got together with Penny? Could being with her have denied him the chance to be with someone else? If it wasn't for Jacob there was no question what he would do, but the boy's very existence depended on the monumental choice facing him and he couldn't take it lightly. He looked to the bracelet for an opinion, thinking about first one option and then the other.

It remained inert, not wanting to get involved. Clearly, although the question of whether or not Jacob existed or not seemed vitally important to Keith, the bracelet didn't deem it of any significance. That was a bit disheartening and made him feel rather small and unimportant in the grand scheme of things. It also suggested his son would never amount to anything worthwhile. It seemed that he had been given a free choice and it was an agonising one.

Perhaps he needed to get away for a few days to take his mind off it. Before he had clapped eyes on Penny, he had already been planning to broach something with Jerry. Returning to the ever-smoky newsroom, he sought out his boss who for once was leaning back in his chair in a relaxed pose, suggesting it was a slow news day.

"Ah, young Keith," he said in an unusually affable tone, before taking a draw on his pipe. "What can I do for you?"

"It's about JR," said Keith confidently. "I know who shot him."

"Come off it, of course you don't. Nobody does. The bookies are even offering odds on it. They wouldn't risk that if someone had inside information, would they?"

"Somebody does. The people who filmed it. The episode's going out on Saturday. You can't tell me it's not in the can already."

"Of course it's in the can. Under lock and key, with maximum security. They're even having the episode specially flown into the UK under armed guard."

"What if I said I had a cousin who knows someone in the film crew who was there the day it was filmed?" asked Keith. This was total bullshit but he deemed it worth a try. But Jerry was ahead of him on this one.

"Nice try, but that won't wash, I'm afraid. Haven't you heard? They've filmed about ten different endings with every possible suspect shooting him. Even the cast don't know!"

"Well, I do know. It's Kristin." Keith said this with the utmost confidence. Having now reacquainted himself with the show, he could even picture it. "Put that in Saturday's paper, and you'll put millions on the circulation."

"Keith, they may call you the oracle around here for your uncannily accurate predictions but I'm not risking our paper's reputation on one of your hunches."

"Our paper has a reputation?" said Keith cheekily. "Who knew? Anyway, I do have one more idea."

"Come on, then, let's hear it," said Jerry. "And then we'll clock off for lunch and go down the pub. There's not a lot going on here today."

"Did you know that the episode is going out a day earlier in America? Friday night there, Saturday night here. So how about this? I fly out to New York tonight, book into a hotel, watch the episode as it goes out, and then ring you with confirmation on Friday night. You put it in the paper on Saturday – bingo!"

"Why would I need to fly you all the way to New York to do that?" replied Jerry. "We do have contacts across the pond, you know. I could get any of them to ring me with the very same information. But I'm not going to."

"And why ever not?"

"Firstly, because we've made an agreement with all the other papers and broadcasters that we're going to have a news blackout so as not to spoil the surprise."

"Since when has that ever stopped you?" asked Keith, but Jerry ignored the question.

"Secondly, I think you've forgotten about the time difference between the UK and America. By the time the show goes out there, we'll be well into the small hours here and way past our publishing deadline. So, to conclude, it's not happening."

"Fine," said Keith, who could see that he was defeated. "I bet you a tenner it was Kristin, though."

"You're on," said Jerry, taking another puff on his pipe. "Since she is 4/1 at the bookies, I'll be more than happy to take a tenner off you at even money. And now I suggest we repair to the pub for a liquid lunch."

Alas, their planned refreshments would have to be put on hold. Just as they were preparing to leave, Gordon came rushing over, clutching a printout from the Telex machine.

"Hold the front page, boss," he said. "This press release has just come in from Yorkshire Police. It seems the Ripper's killed again."

"Bloody hell," said Keith, furious with both the police and himself for not preventing this latest murder. Why had they ignored him?

Rapidly, the newsroom once again took on the frenzied atmosphere it always did when a major news story broke. For the moment, all talk of *Dallas* seemed trivial by comparison. With his hands full for the rest of the afternoon, he was able to put Penny to the back of his mind for the time being. Later at home, reflecting on the events of the day, he reached a decision.

He was frustrated, angry, and more than a little guilty about the Ripper situation. Despite his best efforts, he seemed powerless to do anything about him. The fate of him and Penny, however, was very much in his own hands. Unfortunately, what seemed like a straightforward task on paper turned out to be more difficult than he had thought.

The basic plan had been simply not to ask her out as well as avoiding the typesetting room. This turned out not to be enough. On Friday evening, in the pub across the road, he was unwinding with Jimmy amid a lively crowd of drinkers when she came in with a couple of the other girls she worked with. Any hopes of avoiding her were dashed as she made a beeline straight for him.

"Hello! It's Keith, isn't it? I saw you in the office the other day. I'm Penny. So, are you going to buy me a drink then?"

All the while she was saying this, she was looking up adoringly at him and standing well inside his personal space. She couldn't have made it any more obvious that she was into him. In any other circumstances he would have played along, flashing his charismatic charm, but today he needed to do the complete opposite. Avoiding her had not worked so he would have to quickly implement a new plan. He needed to ensure she never wanted anything to do with him ever again and the best way he could think of was to behave in the most loathsome manner possible. Taking a deep breath, he mustered the harshest response he could think of on the spur of the moment.

"No thanks," he said matter-of-factly and, with not a glimmer on his face to suggest he might be joking, added, "I only bang brunettes."

If anyone was shocked by this, it was Jimmy. He had never heard Keith speak to a woman in such a way. Penny, surprisingly, was undeterred by Keith's rejection and merely counterattacked with the sassy retort, "Just as well I'm not a natural blonde, then, eh? Maybe you'll find out later?"

"I doubt it," said Keith. "No offence, sweetheart, but you'd need to lose at least a stone before I'd even consider banging you."

"Keith!" exclaimed Jimmy. "What's the matter with you?" Turning to Penny, he added, "I do apologise for my friend. He's not normally like this."

"I am normally like this," said Keith, "and I don't shag slappers. You look like a slapper to me."

With her complete lack of makeup and demure attire of sweater and dark trousers, it was a completely unjustifiable slur, but it did the trick.

"You arsehole," she said.

"Good job you found out now, before it went any further, eh?" said Keith.

"Men like you disgust me," replied Penny, her bubbly persona having rapidly deflated like a popped balloon. "And I thought you were nice."

"You don't know how wrong you were," said Keith. "Now do me a favour and piss off."

"No, Keith, why don't you piss off?" said Jimmy, who had been watching the scene in disbelief and had now, against all past form, decided to stand up to him for once. "This is uncalled for."

"You're right, it is," said Penny, before adding, "Sorry I didn't catch your name."

"Jimmy," he replied, face brightening up that a woman in Keith's presence had acknowledged his existence for once.

"Well, why don't you buy me a drink instead, then, Jimmy," she suggested, "and we'll leave this tosser to his own devices."

"I wouldn't if I were you, Jimmy," said Keith. "You've no idea what you're letting yourself in for."

"I'll be the judge of that, mate," said Jimmy. "Come on, Penny, let's go to the other end of the bar."

Keith watched them go, feeling extremely uncomfortable with the situation. He had never treated a woman like that before in his life, despite his philandering ways. If he had heard another bloke talking like that to a lady, he would probably have punched them out. But this was a uniquely unusual scenario that he had been forced to handle in the heat of the moment and it hadn't been a particularly pleasant experience.

Her going off with Jimmy was a bit unexpected. What if by some strange quirk of fate, the two of them got involved with each other? Might Jimmy end up going through all the same shit as him? She wouldn't be interested in him, would she? No one else ever was. But if she wasn't, why had she gone off with him? She had two other friends in the pub she could have gone back to.

His concerns were heightened when Jimmy didn't come home that night, which left Keith to spend Saturday on his own. It was the day the identity of JR's shooter was to be revealed, not that any of his attempts to get the story into the newspaper had come to anything. It had reached the point where Jerry had told him to shut up about it or start looking for another job. Still, there was one consolation. On Monday he would be taking a tenner off the baldy, pipe-smoking old fool.

When Jimmy did return to the house, his suspicions were confirmed when he saw that he was accompanied by Penny. And what did the bracelet have to say about it? Not what he was expecting at all. It was glowing green. Could this be what was supposed to have happened all along? Had Jimmy getting with Penny instead of him been the correct route for the timeline? It was a development he hadn't seen coming, and he wished he hadn't behaved quite so badly the previous evening now as her presence in the flat made for a very uncomfortable evening.

As soon as *Dallas* ended, with Kristin finally unmasked, he was off to the pub on his own. Jimmy and Penny were all over each other on the sofa and he couldn't get out of the house quickly enough.

December 1980

"Are you serious?" asked Ted, eyes widening in shock and astonishment. Keith had come up with some stunning revelations over the past year and he knew not to take them lightly. But this one had really hit home.

"Yes," said Keith. "John Lennon's going to be murdered, next week, in New York. By some nutter called Mark Chapman."

"Then you have to stop him!" urged Ted frantically. "The loss to the world would be incalculable. It's not just the music, he's been such a force for peace too."

"I'm not sure I can," replied Keith gloomily. The bracelet, which as ever was moving in mysterious ways, had made it all too clear with its red-light warnings that he was to leave well alone every time he had thought about it.

"Of course you can!" urged Ted. "Do you know where and when it's going to happen?"

"Not in great detail," admitted Keith. "Only that it happened early in December 1980. I don't even remember the precise date. So I've got nothing to go on."

"But you know the name of the man who did it?"

"Yes, but how is that going to help me?"

"Alert the authorities in New York. Get them to stop him."

"Like they're going to take any notice!" said Keith. "Look what happened with Yorkshire Police here. I gave them all the information they needed to arrest Sutcliffe

233

yet he is still at large. What chance have we got trying the same with a police force in another country? None."

It seemed there was little he could do. If one of the tasks he had been sent to 1980 for was to save Lennon then the bracelet would have supplied him with the precise location, time and means to intervene. It had not. The message was clear; leave well alone.

But why? If Lennon was a force for peace, why must the timeline be maintained in this way? Could his anti-war support be the problem? Although peace was always preferable to war, many had speculated on how history might have turned out differently in certain scenarios. What would have happened, for example, if Britain had continued the policy of appeasement in 1939? Or America had decided not to enter the same war? Sometimes peace was not the best policy and the meek who supported it went to the wall. It wasn't inconceivable that Lennon's continued presence in the world, despite his good intentions, might lead to some unforeseen consequences later.

"Mind your backs, chaps," said one of the girls from the typesetting pool, who was standing on a stepladder behind them, reaching up to attach one end of a lengthy piece of silver tinsel to the ceiling. As she did, there was a wolf whistle from Gordon across the room as her skirt rode up, revealing a generous helping of thigh. The girls from the other office had come into the newsroom to put up the Christmas decorations, something that would never have happened if it had been left to the men.

Across the room, he could see Jimmy handing Penny bits of Blu Tack as she also assisted in the effort to brighten up the place. He had been following her around like a devoted puppy after the two of them had quickly become an item. Keith wasn't sure how he felt about that at all. It was a relief to be free of the shackles that his relationship with her had cast him into, but he had bargained without her getting together with Jimmy. It seemed she was destined to remain connected to his life whether he wanted that or not.

Once the girl had moved on to the next part of the room, Ted and Keith finished their conversation.

"There's nothing I can do even if I wanted to," said Keith. "I can just imagine Jerry's response if I ran this by him. He already thinks I've got some sort of obsession with trying to get to New York on expenses. And even if I could get there, I probably wouldn't be able to do anything. I don't know enough about it."

"I still have contacts in the States from my days in the intelligence services," replied Ted.

"You've got contacts everywhere, Ted. The criminal underworld, FBI, MI5. It wouldn't surprise me if you didn't have a hotline straight to the Kremlin as well."

"I have a friend in New York who's high up in the CIA. You can't object to me trying him, can you? I mean, we can't just sit here and do nothing until Lennon gets blown away, can we?"

"Go ahead," said Keith, noting that there was no negative response from the bracelet. That meant Ted's phone call would probably achieve nothing, and so it proved. Less than a week later, news of Lennon's shooting stunned the world, just as it had before.

"Looking on the bright side," said Jimmy, as they shared a lunchtime pint the following Tuesday. "At least his death's going to keep St. Winifred's School Choir off the Christmas number one."

"I'm not sure he's even going to manage that," said Keith, over the hubbub in the busy pub. It was nine days until Christmas and the journalists of Fleet Street were already demob happy. December was effectively one long piss-up for them.

"You heard the new chart earlier," said Jimmy. "He's gone straight to number one."

Jimmy was referring to Lennon's current hit, *Starting Over*, which had been going down the chart, after peaking in the top ten a few weeks ago. Now, in the wake of his death, it had rebounded straight to the top spot.

"Yes, but I don't think he's going to stay there," said Keith. There had been some truly horrific Christmas number ones over the years, and in his eyes, this one was the worst of the lot; a bunch of sickly-sweet schoolchildren singing 'There's No One Quite Like Grandma'. Even Mr Blobby wasn't as bad as this, and that was saying something.

"Anyway, are you looking forward to the Christmas party on Friday?" asked Jimmy.

"Of course I am," said Keith, and he certainly was. Time was running out for him in 1980, and the party was about the only thing he had left to look forward to. His memories of these annual debauched events were hazy, clouded as they were by alcohol, but their outrageous nature remained etched in his memory. 'Wild' would be putting it mildly. Nothing was off limits.

He wasn't to be disappointed. It was the trend at the time for companies to hold their Christmas parties on the premises rather than hire a venue. On the day in question everyone pitched in, the women supplying the food, and the men bringing the booze. Gordon, who had been a part-time DJ in his younger days, provided the sound system, rocking out the newsroom with a mix of current chart hits and Christmas favourites. And for the next few hours, everyone got incredibly drunk.

Every cliché about such parties was fulfilled, from the photocopying of tits and arses to shagging in the stationery cupboard. Kissing was plentiful, almost obligatory it seemed, and there wasn't a miserable face in sight. It was a far cry from the way the world would later become when virtually every attendee at this party would have found themselves hauled in front of HR on Monday morning.

Here, in 1980, no one had even heard the term Human Resources. There was a small department called Personnel which was responsible for hiring and firing and very little else. There were no endless pointless courses to send people on. Any training that was done was relevant to the job and done on the job. As for the party, no one was going to go complaining about being offended by anything afterwards. They were all too busy having a good time.

Drunk as he was, Keith was able to reflect on all this as he looked around the room. People were much happier just doing what they wanted. Here they were able to interact freely, with no social media, and no offence culture. This was the one day a year when everyone let their hair down after a hard year's work and all in attendance were loving every minute of it. Keith much preferred the freedom of this environment to the risk-averse, mollycoddling, straitjacketed society to which he would soon return.

What would he find waiting for him when he got back? How different was his life in 2020 going to be from how it had been before? Would he still have a job? Would he have married someone else? With the changes he had made via his interactions with Nathalie and Penny, anything was possible.

Christmas Day dawned and he found himself spending the day alone. Jimmy and Penny were now so wrapped up in each other they couldn't bear to be apart and had gone to have Christmas dinner with her parents. *Rather you than me*, thought Keith, remembering how dreadful his mother-in-law's cooking had been. She had perfected the art of cremating roast potatoes and parsnips, whilst conversely undercooking the meat. Every time he had eaten there it had led to unpleasant bathroom experiences the following day. And it wasn't just that, they were utterly boring too, him banging on about his collection of military memorabilia all the time and her about her knitting. He was glad to be out of it.

He planned to gorge himself on food, drink, and Christmas television. He wasn't wasting time on cooking anything. Instead, he had stocked up with all manner of provisions that didn't require any effort beyond opening the fridge door. He had a selection of cold meats and cheeses, bread, crisps, sausage rolls, pork pies and a large box of Milk Tray. On the booze front, there was beer, wine, and a selection of spirits. In the unlikely event of unexpected well-wishers turning up, he would have plenty to offer them.

Thankfully he remained undisturbed, which enabled him to enjoy a day of sheer indulgence. Christmas TV had been a big deal when he was younger, with the main channels pulling out all the stops. It was a far cry from the insipid fare of later years where it seemed all the BBC could be bothered to do was bang out a couple of *Call the Midwife* and *Mrs Brown's Boys* Christmas specials. He wasn't interested in the former and positively despised the latter.

In 1980 there was almost too much to choose from, and that was with just three television channels. Well, two really, as there was bugger all on BBC2. Despite this, he still had to buy two separate TV magazines to get the listings for both channels. It was the *Radio Times* for BBC1 and the *TV Times* for ITV. This seemed crazy compared to the future when he could buy one magazine with listings for hundreds of channels.

Less was more, it seemed, and there was more that he wanted to watch on just these two channels than he could reasonably cope with, and lacking a video recorder, he needed to make a choice. This had all been done the day before when he had sat down with the magazines and assiduously studied both, planning his viewing with the help of a yellow Staedtler highlighter pen.

The morning viewing began with *Runaround* presented by Mike Reid, followed by the children's film, *Digby, the Biggest Dog in the World*. This looked incredibly dated to Keith's twenty-first-century eyes but he couldn't deny it brought back nostalgic memories and anything with Spike Milligan in it was always a bonus. Both were on ITV and then it was over to the BBC for the afternoon for *Top of the Pops*, which had some tremendous acts on but was marred by the inevitable presence of the odious Savile.

After the Queen, he stayed on BBC1 for *20,000 Leagues Under the Sea*, followed by *The Paul Daniels Magic Christmas Show*. Then it was time for that great Christmas staple, the Bond film, over on ITV. This was a slight disappointment as it was *The Man with the Golden Gun* which wasn't one of his favourites. He would have preferred a Connery, but he enjoyed it more than he expected. *The Morecambe and Wise Christmas Show* followed, during which he dozed off, very much full to the brim with Christmas spirit. When he woke up, there was static on the television which had closed down for the night, so he took himself off to bed and slept until lunchtime the following day.

When Jimmy and Penny burst in, full of the joys of a young couple in love, he was sitting watching the Boxing Day horse racing from Kempton Park. They were full of themselves, enthusing about the wonderful Christmas Day they had just enjoyed and showing off the gifts they had bought each other – a new digital watch for him, and a heart-shaped necklace for her. Keith found it nauseating but it did not stop him from feeling a tinge of jealousy at the situation. It wasn't about her. He hadn't wanted her, after all, so there was no reason he should feel jealous that Jimmy was now with her instead.

It was more about the situation. The two of them were far happier than he and Penny had ever been. What did that say about him? he wondered, leading to a lot of soul-searching. Jimmy was treating her with respect, far more than he had ever given her, and it showed in the way they acted together. Why was that? Was it because Jimmy had been so luckless with women in the past that he was making a superhuman effort because he feared he might lose her again?

Keith had never experienced that problem, at least not in his younger years. He had been able to pick up and drop women at his leisure, and he was beginning to think that was a bad thing. He hadn't had to try, so he hadn't made any effort. If a woman got on his nerves, he just dropped her and picked up another one. It had been just like one big game where he was the winner and Jimmy was a perennial loser. But it hadn't done him any good in the long run. That was why despite being in the public eye, he was on his own and lonely by the time he passed sixty, with little prospect of that ever changing.

It was a daunting and depressing thought, and he found it a great struggle to get through the rest of Boxing Day and the evening in the face of their exuberance. Even going to bed provided little relief. Shortly afterwards, he suffered the misery of listening to them having noisy, happy sex from the room next door while he lay alone. How many times in the past had this position been reversed? All those times he had brought women back to the flat while Jimmy was on his own in the next room, knowing he could hear and not caring. Almost revelling in it, to be honest. Now their positions were reversed, he did not like it at all.

What had he achieved here in 1980, quite frankly? Sure, he had helped a few people out, saved a few lives, tried and failed to save a few others. But in terms of his

241

personal life, it seemed like he had made things worse, not better. As the empty days between Christmas and New Year trickled away, his growing dread at the thought of going back became overwhelming. He had never felt so low.

Then, on the 30th of December, everything changed. He was back at work, putting together a story about a proposed breakfast television service, when he got a call from reception telling him he had a visitor. He wasn't expecting anyone and couldn't for the life of him think who it might be. When he entered the reception area and saw who had come to see him, his heart soared. He couldn't think of anyone else he would rather it have been.

Sitting on the sofa, just as she had been the day she had first come in almost nine months before, was Rachel Summers, looking more beautiful than ever. As soon as she saw Keith, she leapt up, rushing across to him, eyes sparkling brightly, full to the brim with happiness to see him. To his great delight, she wrapped her arms around him and gave him a huge, warm hug.

"Rachel!" he exclaimed, as they pulled back from each other. "You came back!"

"I certainly did. I promised I would and today's the day."

"I can't tell you how incredible it is to see you," he said, feeling happy for the first time in days. "You must tell me all your news – shall we go for a drink?"

"I was hoping you might say that!" she said. "Same place as last time?"

He didn't even bother going back to his desk to get his jacket or tell anyone where he was going. The weather was mild and Jerry had the whole of the Christmas period off so no one was going to be checking up on him. What did it matter, anyway? He was going to be out of here in a couple of days and there was no way he was going to miss this chance to spend some time with Rachel.

She was dressed in a chunky green jumper and tight jeans, as were becoming popular. The flares still prevalent at the start of the year had all but disappeared from the streets of London. Fashion moved fast in the 1980s.

At the same table as last time, with the same double vodka, she lit up a B&H and filled Keith in on what she had been doing since they last met.

"I got straight A's in my exams, securing my place at Cambridge to study medicine," she explained. "I'm living in the halls there and I have to say, I've been having an amazing time. You were so right about this being the best thing for me to do. I don't know what I was thinking before. If it hadn't been for you, I don't know what might have happened."

Just like before, she began blowing out smoke rings, adding to the cloud of smoke already hanging in the air.

"I'm so pleased it's working out for you," he replied, adding his own Marlboro fumes to the fug. He was going to have to give this up soon. There would be no more smoking in pubs where he was going. And his sixty-plus body wouldn't appreciate it either.

"You said that it would and I trusted you, even though I had my doubts. But then, as the months passed and all those things you told me came true, I knew I was right to believe in you. Who would have thought Ronald Reagan would become president, for a start? I mean, it's not that I didn't believe you before because my gut feeling convinced me you were telling the truth. The one thing you didn't properly explain before was how you knew all this stuff. It's been bugging me ever since and I was hoping maybe you would tell me now."

Keith thought about it. Other than Ted, no one else knew about his ability to see the future, and even he didn't know the whole story. He had no qualms at all about telling Rachel. His work here was done so what harm would it do? The bracelet wasn't flashing any red lights at him right now so why not?

"I will," said Keith, wondering what the best way to explain it all would be. "I'm a time traveller. From the future. Well, my mind is, anyway."

"What do you mean, your mind is?" she asked, perplexed.

"OK, I didn't put that very well," said Keith. "What you are looking at is the body of me, as I always have been, in 1980. But my mind is from my future self, sent here from forty years in the future. I've seen everything that's happened this year before, as well as every year after this until 2019."

"But why? And how?"

"I don't fully understand it myself. I met a woman who passed on an ancient bracelet which sent me back in time. I'm here for a year to keep things on track, then

I pass the bracelet to the next person. It's a calendar year, so my time's almost up. Tomorrow night, I'll be heading off to the year 2020 and I can't tell you it's a prospect I'm relishing. By then, I'm in my sixties, I've just lost my job and the future's not looking promising."

"If that's the case, we'd better make sure you make the best of the time you've got left, then," she replied, captivating him with her eyes. He gazed back, not wanting to break whatever this was, before she stubbed her cigarette out in the ashtray, got up, leant across the table, and kissed him.

It was a kiss like none he had experienced for a long time. Rather than just being a prelude to sex, which was what every other kiss he'd had in 1980 had been, this felt pure and full of genuine emotion. For someone so casual and jaded about such matters, who had recently wondered whether he had a single romantic bone in his body, it was a watershed moment. He fell for her, there and then.

When Rachel broke off the kiss and sat back in her seat, everything had changed between them. There was a charge like static electricity in the air and it was not down to physical attraction alone. The only thing taking the edge of it was that he had been here almost a year and now this magical moment had arrived, with less than a day and a half to go.

"Wow," was all he could think of to say.

"Snap," she replied, as they maintained eye contact across the table again, each unable to look away. It was as if words weren't needed anymore; they were communicating purely with their eyes.

It was the same when they went to bed, back at his house, later that afternoon. Before, he had barely looked at a woman's face in bed, he just got on and did the business. Now he couldn't take his eyes off her. Afterwards, as they cuddled up enjoying the warmth of each other as the cold December dusk fell, he could honestly say he had never felt closer to another human being in his whole life.

"So, what happens now?" he eventually said, as they lay together.

"What do you want to happen now?" she asked, turning yet again to gaze at him. All he wanted to do was drown in those eyes and never look away. And to think of the fate that might have awaited those beautiful eyes if the timeline had been allowed to follow its original course. He could quite happily have frozen this moment and stayed here in eternity. But as always, there were practicalities to consider.

"I want to stay with you forever," he said. "But I can't. I'm going away tomorrow night, and then I'm going to lose you."

"But will you, though? I mean, when your mind goes back to the future, your body will still be here. Surely, you'll remember all this, won't you? You'll still be you."

"I don't know," he admitted. "I'm not sure if that's how it works. All I know is that me – as in this me, won't be here anymore. Even if I leave an identical copy behind."

"Then, like I said before, let's not waste this precious time we have together. And after tomorrow, we'll just have to see what happens, won't we?"

"I guess we will," he said, as she propped herself up on her right elbow and leaned forward to kiss him once again.

January 2020

"Wake up, sleepyhead. You're going to be late for work."

Keith's eyes slowly fluttered open, recognising the voice but unable to respond right away. He felt befuddled about where he was as if he were halfway between the dream world and reality. As he tried to get a grip on his thoughts, the woman in bed next to him flicked on the lamp on her bedside table, illuminating the room in a low light before turning back to face him.

If there ever was such a thing as a sight for sore eyes, then surely this must be it. He recognised her instantly, even though she was four decades older than the last time he had seen her. It was the eyes that did it, as piercing and alluring as ever and looking at him from a face, that although weathered with age, was still as beautiful to him as it had ever been.

"Rachel?" Keith managed to stammer, his heart fluttering as he realised that something he hadn't even dared dream might be possible could now be a reality. Were they still together in the future? Was he finally in the happy relationship he had never thought possible with anyone?

She smiled warmly, her hand reaching out to gently stroke his cheek. "Keith, it really is me. Today's the day you've come back, isn't it? Just like we talked about?"

Keith sat up in bed, thinking back to their last night together in 1980. He had elaborated further on the nature of the bracelet and they speculated about what would happen when his mind returned to the future. All they knew for sure was that the next time he woke up he fully expected it to be the first day of 2020. Judging by what he had seen so far, that was exactly what had happened. And here she was, waiting for him, having remembered for all these years.

"Yes, today's the day. But how is it you come to be here now? I mean, that last conversation, the night before I left, was forty years ago."

"I know and we've been together ever since," she explained excitedly, eager to fill him in on everything he had missed. "We've built a whole life together. Don't you remember any of it? Have a look around. This is our home – do you recognise any of it?"

As Keith looked around the room, he could see that it was very different to the flat in Fulham in which he had spent the last few years. This room was far more spacious, and well-furnished and had luxurious red curtains covering what looked like bay windows. The architecture within the room suggested it was of Georgian construction. Overall, the room exuded warmth, contentment, and wealth. Places like this didn't come cheap in London, if that was where they were.

His eyes were drawn to a large framed picture on the wall of himself, Rachel, and two young women. It was a classic family portrait which surely could only mean one thing.

"Are they…?" he began, struggling to find the right words.

"Yes, Keith. They're our daughters and they're amazing. We've had a wonderful life and raised a beautiful family. Perhaps you'll remember it all in time. Just like your other self, did."

"My other self?"

"Yes. You were a little confused after you went back to the future in 1981. Your memories of the year you had spent in the past were hazy and you were not yourself for the first week or two. But eventually, the two halves of you merged back together and it all made sense."

"Like my past mind and future mind merging?" suggested Keith. "It feels as if there are two different versions of me now. The one you've lived with for the last forty years. And this one, who has just jumped here from 1980."

"I imagine it's all going to be a little confusing for a while, but for now, much as I would love to spend the morning with you, you've got to get to work. You had planned to have the day off bearing in mind we weren't sure whether you would be in a fit state of mind to go in, but unfortunately your cover presenter cried off sick yesterday and they called you back in for this morning."

His circumstances might have changed but it sounded as if work might still be as it was. He could see from the gap in the curtains that it was still dark outside, so he reached over to his bedside table where he could see his iPhone, the same one he had possessed previously. Waking it up, he could see that it was only 5am on New Year's Day. He must still be presenting the breakfast show.

"I still work at the radio station, then?" he asked.

"At ChatFM?" she replied. "Of course."

"And I didn't get sacked yesterday?"

"Of course not," she said. "You've just been voted broadcaster of the year."

"What, really? Me? What did the Twitterati have to say about that?"

"Nothing bad, as far as I know. Everyone loves you, Keith."

"Blimey," he said, wondering what on earth had brought about this change. Was it the love of a good woman? Perhaps it had left him with a better disposition. And to think, he had been convinced when he scuppered his relationship with Penny that he wasn't the settling-down type. The current situation suggested he had been way off with that assumption. Still, he could think about that later, for now he needed to hope that his job wasn't going to come with any complications.

"Listen, I'm a bit worried about work," he said. "It appears that my life has changed a lot."

"Not as much as mine," she said. "According to you, I died in 1984 in your old timeline."

"Indeed," he said, aware that he knew very little about her new life. "This might sound odd, but what do you do?"

"I'm a senior surgeon at one of London's top eye hospitals. I specialise in pioneering new and improved techniques to restore sight to those who would have had no hope of seeing again without the work we do."

"That's amazing," said Keith. "And incredibly rewarding too." He looked around the room again. No wonder they could afford to live in such a luxurious home.

"And it's all down to you, Keith. I'm so glad I listened to you all those years ago and so grateful to whoever sent you back through time to warn me. I owe them, and you, my life."

"It wasn't just down to me. Ultimately, it was your decision."

"And I made the right one, thanks to you," she replied, as Keith wondered what else might have changed.

"That's got me thinking, what about the rest of the world? Is that all different too? I mean, who's Prime Minister?"

"Boris Johnson."

"And Brexit's still a big deal?"

"People go on about nothing else."

"Phew!" he said. "Not because of Brexit or Johnson, but because the world sounds as if it is the same as I remember it. I'll probably be a bit rusty when I go on the air later but hopefully, I'll know roughly what I'm talking about. If I can muddle through the first day things should be alright. I'll have a good browse through the news on my phone on the way in, just to check everything else is as it should be."

"You'd better get up, then," she said. "We'll talk more later. And, since you probably don't remember, I had better remind you that we're going out for a meal tonight with Jimmy and Penny for his birthday."

"What, they're still together too?" he asked, with an astounded look on his face.

"They've been married for thirty-seven years. Three years longer than us."

"Wow," he replied, noticing the ring on his finger for the first time. He got up and swung his legs out of bed, at which point he noticed another change.

He was much fitter and thinner than he had been before his trip back to the past. He felt more energetic too – not in comparison to his 1980 self but compared to how he had been when he left 2019. Perhaps that was another thing that could be attributed to his improved domestic circumstances. If he was happy with Rachel he probably ate better rather than scoffing takeaways and swigging booze all the time.

They drank coffee together, and then he kissed her goodbye, still scarcely believing her being with him was real before he departed into the frosty January morning. As he had planned, he spent his time on the way to work on the Tube reacquainting himself with the news. Twice he was interrupted by fans who recognised him. This didn't bother him at all; it was nice to know he was still someone in this world.

Nothing had changed as far as he could see so he took the chance to look up a couple of things that had been bugging him. He was disappointed to discover that Jimmy Savile had never been brought to justice in his lifetime. However, he was relieved to discover that Peter Sutcliffe had been caught just two days into 1981. He wasn't sure if the information he had given to Yorkshire Police had helped or not. He couldn't remember if that date had changed since his trip back in time. But either way, at least he had tried and Sutcliffe had been locked up ever since.

Reassured that the world was as it should be and that his circumstances were greatly improved, he sat back and relaxed. Suddenly here he was, at the dawn of a new decade, with plenty to look forward to. Meeting his two daughters for a start. He felt sad that he had missed them growing up, but if what Rachel had said was true, perhaps he would remember in time.

He still felt bad about Jacob but maybe Penny had other children with Jimmy. It was something he had neglected to ask Rachel before. There was a lot of catching up to do but that was fine. He would be home by lunchtime and then they could spend the whole afternoon together.

The office building was just as he had left it, towering over Canary Wharf. He was greeted by Barry, who was the notoriously rude security guard who manned the front desk.

"Good morning, Mr Diamond, and what rubbish are we going to be spouting on the air this morning?" said the ageing, white-haired ex-military man, who considered insulting every single person who entered the building to be part of his job description.

"Oh, just a story about how disgracefully overpaid London's security guards are," replied Keith, who always enjoyed the cut-and-thrust of a bit of banter with Barry.

"Just as well, I'm leaving then, isn't it?" said Barry, much to Keith's disappointment as a bit of a laugh with him was part of his morning routine. "I'm off to pastures new, in Oxford. Got a job at a big retail place. I'll be closer to the family, decent hours, and as much tea as I can drink. And no jumped-up tosspot radio presenters and celebrity guests to annoy me."

"Well, I hope they appreciate your off-the-wall style in Oxford. It's a bit of an acquired taste."

"They'll do as they're told, just like they do here. Now get yourself into that lift and up to your studio. You don't want to be late for your listeners. That's if you have any."

Keith made his way to the lift which would take him up to the 84th floor. Barry must have been a very good army officer, considering how easily he got people to do as they were told. Even the Diamond Geezer, who didn't like to be told what to do by anyone. Or at least that used to be the case. He was feeling a lot more at ease with the world today than he had for a long time. Who cared about the nanny state and their stupid rules? Let them get on with it.

When he got up to his floor, it suddenly struck him that he didn't need the toilet. He was normally desperate by this point. It seemed that the bladder problems that had plagued him before had vanished. The more time he spent in this new 2020 version of himself, the more he liked it.

After a year away from the hot seat he was worried he might be a little rusty but as he slipped on his headphones, he realised he was going to slip back into the job effortlessly. Everything was going to be fine. The only thing he wasn't sure about was his style. Was this version of him as abrasive as the old one? Rachel had said everybody loved him. What sort of level should he pitch the show at?

He decided to tone things down just a little, staying controversial but without too much of the Diamond Geezer spiel. This seemed to be going well but then, during a break in proceedings, he got a message from Tom that he was wanted upstairs after the show. A sense of déjà vu hit him, remembering what had happened before. Was history about to repeat itself?

When he opened the door to see Nathalie standing there, looking identical to before in her tailored suit, for a moment he feared the worst. Then he thought back to the time she had spent with him on her work experience in 1980. That must count for something, mustn't it? Nervous and eager to find out, he seized the initiative and blurted, "Nathalie! How wonderful to see you again."

She smiled, but unlike the twisted sneer contorted by thoughts of revenge that had betrayed her intentions before, this time all he saw was genuine warmth.

"You too, Keith. It's been too long. Over forty years. You know, I'm amazed you remember me."

"Of course I do!" he said. "You haven't changed a bit."

"You're too kind, Keith. I'm sure at fifty-five I can't be as fresh-faced as I was at fifteen."

"Well, you look amazing for your age, that's all I can say," he replied, doing his utmost not to come across as too obvious. Telling her she hadn't changed after forty years had been pushing it.

"You're not looking so bad yourself," she said. "I'm so glad you've come up. I can't tell you how much I've been looking forward to this meeting."

"Yes, well, speaking of which, it is somewhat of a surprise. Where's Douglas?"

He was playing along, trying to pretend he didn't know what was going on. Doubtless Douglas had been put out to pasture, just like before.

"He's taking early retirement with a nice pension," she said. "He left yesterday. I'm sure you must have heard the rumours about the takeover."

"I did hear a few rumblings on the old bush telegraph."

"Indeed. Well, the long and the short of it is that my company, Lone Wolf Media, have bought ChatFM and we've got big changes planned."

"Oh," said Keith, wondering if even after all this he was still destined for the chop. He had never heard of Lone Wolf. He was sure she had said that she worked for Rainbow Media before. There was no sense in pussyfooting around it, he might as well just come out with it.

"So, am I out on my ear?"

"Goodness, no. Whyever would you think that? I've come here because for years I have thought that I would never be able to repay you enough for what you did for me when I came to do my work experience. That newsroom was a total shock to my rather naïve young mind. I had no idea before that men could be that vile. And you were the only one who was different. You took me under your wing and looked after me."

"Oh, it was nothing," said Keith modestly.

"It was a lot more than nothing, and you know it. You made the effort to teach me things and treat me like a human being, as opposed to the rest of them who saw me as a piece of meat. You even took me to the Motor Show and the Tory Party Conference. And, to your great credit, you didn't take advantage when I...you know..."

"Tried to kiss me?"

"Exactly. For the past forty years, I've been waiting for a chance to thank you properly and now that day has come. I think you're going to like what I have to say."

"Let's hear it, then," said Keith excitedly. Could this day get any better? It turned out it could.

"I'm the European Regional Vice President of Lone Wolf Media, an American company that runs dozens of radio and television stations. I don't blame you if you haven't heard of us, we aren't that well known yet outside of the United States. Anyway, the company has big plans overseas which includes setting up here in the UK."

"So you're taking over ChatFM?"

"More than that. Very soon, ChatFM will no longer exist."

"So where does that leave me?"

"Allow me to clarify. ChatFM will no longer exist in its current form but in its place will come ChatTV. We're taking over this station, rebranding it, and we are going to bring the Chat format to television. We're putting in a multi-million-pound investment and we want you, Keith Diamond, to be our top star. Primetime TV every weeknight, your own talk show, and numerous other things. There is just one thing, though."

"Which is?"

"I've noticed you're employed here on an ad hoc basis, just being paid by the shift."

"That's right," said Keith, sensing that she was about to make him an offer.

"We can't have that, can we? What if the opposition should try and steal you? So, I've taken the liberty of having our lawyers draw up a contract. You don't have to sign it right now but put it this way. How does a million pounds a year sound?"

Keith had been hoping for something lucrative, but nothing on this scale. It was outstanding, and his jaw dropped accordingly. He had been getting five hundred quid a show from ChatFM. Barely able to speak, he just about managed to stammer out, "It...it sounds amazing!"

"That's what I was hoping you would say. Welcome to Lone Wolf Media. That week you spent looking after me back in 1980 was time well invested, was it not?"

"It certainly was," he said, as Nathalie produced a bottle of champagne and two glasses from the fridge that Douglas had installed precisely for such occasions. He might have gone but it looked like Keith was here to stay.

"Shall we celebrate?" she suggested.

"Just try and stop me!" he replied, as she uncorked the champagne. Soon they were clinking glasses and toasting the future.

And that was pretty much that. His entire life had been completely transformed by the year he had spent in 1980. He had gone to the past with such bad intentions, angry at being moralized at by the bracelet, and embittered about all the things that had gone wrong in his life. But despite his misgivings, he had overcome that negative start and made a proper go of it. And now, with both Rachel and Nathalie, it seemed he had been rewarded in ways he could scarcely have imagined.

That afternoon he met Elizabeth and Brooke, his grown-up daughters, for the first time. But as soon as he clapped eyes on them there was a sense of familiarity, and a few snippets of memories of their childhood began to filter into his head. It looked like this was the beginning of the merging of his mind with that of the other Keith, just as Rachel had suggested.

That evening, he and Rachel dined in one of the West End's finest restaurants where they celebrated Jimmy's birthday and Keith's new job. Even Penny was nice to him. It seemed she had forgiven him for his disgraceful behaviour that night they had first met properly in the pub. Curious to confirm this, he steered the conversation around to talking about that very night.

With the wine loosening her tongue, she was quite happy to say that she thought he was a complete tosser when she first met him but that he had much improved with age. Just to put the icing on the cake of what had been a perfect day, he discovered that Penny and Jimmy had two sons, and had named one of them Jacob. He knew it wasn't the same Jacob but in some way, it was comforting to imagine that his son from the other timeline still lived on here in some shape or form.

All he had left to do was to pass the bracelet on to the next custodian, who would be travelling back to repeat the same task but in 1981. Who would it be? It could be anyone and if he understood the mechanics of this correctly, he wouldn't find out until the end of the year. He just hoped that whoever it was would make as much of the opportunity as he had.

THE END...but you can meet the next recipient of the bracelet in 1981: A Year in the Life of Nick Taylor.

Also by Jason Ayres
1981: A Year in the Life of Nick Taylor

1981 wasn't a year Nick remembered fondly. His mother was killed in a plane crash, his father ran off with the babysitter, and he was sent to possibly the most horrible school in the world. 2020 ends on a similar note when that babysitter, now his stepmother, can't be bothered to tell him his father is dying until it is too late. To rub salt into the wounds she promptly disinherits him.

Then Nick meets television star Keith Diamond who gives him a bracelet with the power to send him back in time. Arriving in 1981, before the events that shaped his annus horribilis, he realises he now has the power to change the timeline. There's just one problem – no one takes any notice of you when you're only ten.

Join Nick, as he relives the experience of growing up in the 1980s, in this humorous and thought-provoking time travel story. To find out more, check out the links below:

UK: https://www.amazon.co.uk/dp/B0CQ917XXG
US: https://www.amazon.com/dp/B0CQ917XXG

Also by Jason Ayres
1982: A Year in the Life of Wendy Wood

Meet Wendy Wood. The popstar that never was…

In 1982, Wendy Wood was poised on the brink of stardom. Lead singer with talented local band, Velvet Temptation, she was a rising star of the Oxford music scene. Tipped for fame by the music press, success seemed inevitable.

But conflict within the band, a series of betrayals and infidelities, and an unwelcome run of bad luck all played a part in shattering her dreams.

Forty years later, her health failing, Wendy's only comfort is in karaoke nights, where every song is a poignant reminder of what might have been.

Then, out of the blue, she's handed the means to return to the past. Determined to rewrite her destiny, Wendy is steadfast in her pursuit of the fame that once slipped through her fingers.

Join Wendy as she immerses herself in the vibrant music scene of 1982, navigating the complexities of love, ambition, and second chances in this thought-provoking time travel story.

UK: https://www.amazon.co.uk/dp/B0CW1HDT72
US: https://www.amazon.com/dp/B0CW1HDT72

The Time Bubble Collection

The Time Bubble is an epic series, exploring time travel from every possible angle:

UK Link:

https://www.amazon.co.uk/Jason-Ayres/e/B00CQO4XJC/

US Link:

https://www.amazon.com/Jason-Ayres/e/B00CQO4XJC/

The Ronnie and Bernard Adventures

The Ronnie and Bernard Adventures are a pair of humorous novels with mild science fiction and horror elements set in the 1970s. The stories follow the fortunes of two actors from very different backgrounds.

Together they tackle mysteries, travel in time, and negotiate the rocky path of life as jobbing actors, from daytime soaps to panto.

Anyone who remembers the 1970s will love these nostalgic stories looking back at a time when life was simpler, and the world didn't take itself too seriously. Packed with period detail, humour, and references to the era, they are the perfect antidote to modern living.

1) The Crooked Line
2) The Haunted Theatre

UK Link:

https://www.amazon.co.uk/Jason-Ayres/e/B0BR9SMPPY/

US Link:

https://www.amazon.com/Jason-Ayres/e/B0BR9SMPPY/

Follow the Author

To ensure you never miss a release, or to be informed of special deals on Amazon, sign up to follow me on my author page which can be found here:

https://www.amazon.co.uk/stores/Jason-Ayres/author/B00CQO4XJC

For exclusive content from me, regular newsletters and occasional freebies and offers, sign up to my mailing list here:

https://www.jasonayres.co.uk/contact/ or email me directly: jason.ayres@btinternet.com

And of course, there is Facebook, X, and YouTube!

https://www.facebook.com/TheTimeBubble/

https://twitter.com/TheTimeBubble/

https://www.youtube.com/channel/UCg13jmfTUT FCqWWZrPmXqJQ

Finally, if you loved this book and have the time to leave a star rating or review on Amazon, it is always hugely appreciated!

Printed in Dunstable, United Kingdom